SCRUMPTIOUS INDEPENDENCE

MERRIWEATHER ISLAND BOOK TWO

MELISSA WARDWELL

ISBN: 978-1-951839-08-6

Celebrate Lit Publishing

304 S. Jones Blvd #754

Las Vegas, NV, 89107

http://www.celebratelitpublishing.com/

1 John 4:16-19 (NIV) - And so we know and rely on the love God has for us. God is love. Whoever lives in love lives in God, and God in them. This is how love is made complete among us so that we will have confidence on the day of judgment: In this world we are like Jesus. There is no fear in love. But perfect love drives out fear, because fear has to do with punishment. The one who fears is not made perfect in love.

We love because he first loved us.

*M*illions of sand particles engulfed her feet as she stood on the ocean shore with her Gram. Waves crept further and further inland, each one hitting the beach with unattainable force. Behind them, on top of the cliff above, stood a small, white stone cottage, with hurricane shutters propped open to welcome the salty summer breeze. Wildflowers and tall grasses acted as a barrier between the cottage and the rest of the world.

Gram's fragile hand rested in the bend of Beth's arm as the sea spray and sun kissed their skin. Elizabeth watched Gram out of the corner of her eye, as the woman closed her eyes to the wind that blew through her gray hair. A smile spread across her face, forcing the elderly woman's features to soften and reflect her youthful spirit.

"This is where we belong, sugar. There's no other place on earth as heavenly as this spot." The quake in Gram's voice reflected her love for the location.

"Where are we, Gram?"

"You know where this is, look around. This is home." The

woman turned to Beth, giving her a stern look. "When I go to Jesus, bring my body here. Understand?"

Taken aback by the command, Beth pressed for clarification. "But you're not going anywhere. Right, Gram?"

"I love you, my darling child. Never forget that."

Her nerves rattled with the vibration of the phone on the nightstand by Beth's head, jarring her from the dream. With one eye peeking at the neon red light that displayed the time on her bedside clock, she contemplated waiting to check to see who would be crazy enough to send her a text at three in the morning. Closing the eye, she chose to ignore the alert. It was most likely a wrong number. But then, it buzzed again. She opened an eye again to catch her full name in all capital letters on the screen before the backlight went out. She had to respond now.

Before she could get a look at the first text, another one came through. Something was wrong. Her sleepy brain ticked through the list of possibilities.

Daddy's been working long hours. Could he have worked himself into a heart attack?

Mom had a biopsy done on her mole. Could it be cancer? Wait, they wouldn't text me for that.

Maybe Gram? No, she is healthier than I am.

Beth opened the first text from her mother.

Gram is gone. Get yourself together and get home.

Beth lived in a tiny one bed, one bath apartment in the heart of Ann Arbor. It was a place she'd found right after graduation that brought her closer to Gram, but as far as possible from her parents and siblings. As long as she lived here, they had no say in her life.

Mother's second message was her "text yelling" at her for not responding.

The third text was from her oldest sister, Barbara, also yelling at her to wake up and answer.

All Beth could do was look back at those first three words of her mother's original message. *Gram is gone.* What did she mean by that? At eighty-seven, the answer seemed obvious, but Beth had to hear it for herself. She tapped the image of her mother at the top, selected FaceTime, and called.

"Hello," Caroline Stevens' voice came through with her signature blasé tone.

"Mother, what do you mean 'Gram is gone'? Gone where?"

The screen illuminated as her mother turned on her bedside lamp. Irritation flashed in her eyes. Some would say that Caroline Stevens was the perfect wife and mother. Beth chose to see her mother for what she was, a woman concerned with only herself and could not be bothered by the youngest of her family.

"Why did you FaceTime? You know I hate the way I look on this thing. I mean seriously, Elizabeth, it is just completely inconsiderate to call at this time of the morning."

"Mom! What happened to Gram?" Her mother's concern for her looks when this could be a life changing conversation annoyed Beth as much as her phone vibrating had.

"Well, what do you think? Gram passed away. I just got a call from her housekeeper."

Gone. Gram was gone? How could her rock be gone? Beth struggled to inhale as her mother rolled her eyes and the screen went black. Her grandmother, the only one in the family who had her back, who encouraged her dreams to run a restaurant, the one who paid for culinary school ... and she was no longer part of her life. All Beth's mother could do was roll her eyes over it. *Her own mother is gone, and she doesn't care?*

Her lungs burned in her chest as the phone slipped from her grip. When she could grab a breath, it was short and rapid. Her eyes began to ache as the tears began to pool. At last, the sob escaped her and Beth leaned over her crisscrossed legs and screamed in the pillow in her lap. This could not be happening. There was still so much she needed to have Gram around for. There were still so many recipes they needed to perfect. More stories to be shared. Her mom had to have her information wrong, but Beth knew in her heart, it was so.

Images from her dream came to mind and she knew that it was somehow Gram's good-bye.

Journal Entry

May 10th

I can't believe you're gone. I thought we would have more time together. More time to create. More time to laugh. More time to share life. Now I'm sorry I didn't come over last night after work. You asked me to, and I let my busy schedule get in the way. I am so very sorry.

How am I going to do this without you? You have always been there for me, guiding me through each milestone. I'll get through somehow. I promise to make you proud. I'm just not sure how.

Beth

*T*hree days after the funeral, the family sat crowded in the way-too-small office of Gram's lawyer, the garish knotty pine paneling making the room more like a cave than a place of business.

Beth sat in a simple fabric chair in the far corner of the office. Her view of the city skyline gave her something better to look at than the putrid green shag carpet. For as much as Gram paid the attorney, one would think he would be able to afford an office makeover.

When the man himself walked into the room, she figured that probably was not going to happen. His polyester brown suit with the wider-than-normal lapels had been matched with a yellowing buttoned-down shirt. Even the brown leather, pointed-toe shoes indicated his lack of style for the twenty-first century.

A familiar voice spoke in her ear, "Don't be so judgmental, child. Maybe his wife likes to live in the seventies as well." Beth looked around the room in search of Gram's face. Sadly, she had not miraculously appeared.

"Thank you all for coming in. Let me start by saying how

sorry I am that this world had to lose such a lady as your mother." The lawyer, Mr. Nettles, shook Mother's hand as he spoke.

"I think I can speak for everyone by saying the sooner we get this part done, the sooner we can move on," her mother replied in a frigid tone that made Beth's skin crawl.

Her parents sat in high-back chairs in front of the man's desk, while Barbara sat with her husband on the love seat, and Catherine sat with her husband in two more folding chairs on the opposite side of the room from Beth.

Andrew Stevens, her father, checked his phone and pager while the lawyer moved around his desk to take his seat. Her mother, Caroline, sat as stoic as ever, by his side. Not a stitch out of place, her chin upturned, ready for the hefty sum she would soon receive from her mother's estate. Beth and her sisters knew not to expect much more than a few trinkets from their grandmother. Their mother, the sole heir, had made that very clear to them during their growing up years.

Mr. Nettles pressed a button on the little recorder beside him, cleared his throat, and opened the manila envelope. For as much as Granddad and Gram owned in stock, bonds, properties, and who knows what else, Beth expected it to be much thicker than it was. Gram must have kept things simple and clear. All she wanted was the cookbook they created over the years and Gram's Bible. Nothing else mattered to her.

He pressed a button on a small recorder beside him and began. "Elizabeth Dianna Merriweather-Lewis insisted that her will be read immediately after her passing. So, here we are. I will be starting off with her letter to you all and move right on to her wishes."

"My beautiful family," the moment he spoke, his voice disappeared in Beth's mind and Gram's soft, shaky voice replaced it. Beth closed her eyes and soaked in the wonder of the transformation. "I am sorry I had to leave you. I was so looking forward to watching the great-grand-babies grow up. Clearly, God had other plans for me. I can only hope that in my years, I conveyed to you all how proud I am of you. I prayed for you daily in hopes that you will continue to see the hand of the Almighty on your lives. He has surely blessed you abundantly."

"My will does not read as you might have expected. I hope you all can find it in your hearts to forgive me in this. Please, do not show hostility to others who will benefit from my decisions. The choice is not theirs and they were not told ahead of time."

Beth tried not to snicker at her Gram's forwardness. Everyone thought Gram had been starting to lose her mind, but the woman had been sharper than Beth. She'd been a master of observation and could see right through the fake personas some in her family members assumed.

Mr. Nettles proceeded to tell her sisters what they would be receiving—a few pieces of jewelry and other specific household items that were family heirlooms. Beth watched as shock began to register on their faces when the lawyer moved on from their legacies. He then moved on to mother and daddy.

"My darling daughter, you were a light in my life. You are smart, cunning, a true leader." Gram had always said those things about her daughter, but a hint that these were traits used to manipulate others lingered in her tone. "You have done well for yourself in finding a man capable of providing you with the life that resembled that of the one your daddy offered. For this reason, I leave you ..." Mr. Nettles listed pieces of artwork, family treasures, her fine china, and the deed to the lake house in Ludington, Michigan.

"What!? That's it?" The shrill tone made Beth cringe. Her mother was many things, but humble was not one. She wanted the finer things at all times. There was no imitation crab in her salads, only the real thing would do. The woman didn't wear just any jeans, they had to be designer brands.

Beth's father caught her attention with an eye roll as her sisters rushed to their mother's side to console her, bringing her a Kleenex box and speaking in hushed tones. Her overreaction really was laughable. Barbra looked at Beth to get her to join them to help. She knew it would be pointless.

"Who gets the house? The stocks and bonds? The rest of the furnishings?" Her mother sniffled while shooing her two older daughters away. Her father placed his left elbow on the arm of the chair and rested his head in his hand.

"Well," Mr. Nettles looked to Beth, uncertainty and an apology registering in his face. "Ms. Elizabeth Stevens, actually."

Beth's jaw slackened as the room came to a hush. "Me? Why me?"

Gram and Beth spoke of the estate's total value not long ago. She marveled then at all her Gram mapped out for her. Now she saw that the woman was filling her in on what would soon be hers. The details that she would need to pay close attention to as she navigated these next few weeks.

Mr. Nettles stood from his chair, moved around the desk, and approached her with a thick envelope that she had not seen before. He held the eight by eleven, yellow colored envelope to her. "She gave me explicit instructions to hand this directly to you. No courier service, no family members were to be permitted to touch this. Inside, you will find a letter from your grandmother along with deeds, policies, appraisals, stock certificates, and bonds."

Beth's hand shook as she took the offered item. She knew the value these simple papers held. The thought of her own value sent ripples of fear through her. In one swoop of the pen, she was richer than her parents and siblings put together. *Gram, why me?*

She looked to her family for some sort of reassurance that she was still loved by them. Instead, she was met with scathing glares, slack jaws, and a hidden smirk from her daddy. He was the only one left to support her. A lifeline that would love her

8

no matter what, yet she wasn't confident she could always count on him to be available.

It took less than ten minutes for the office to clear out. All except for Beth and Mr. Nettles. Her mother, sisters, and their husbands left within seconds. Her father approached her before following them. He held his hand out to her and wiggled his fingers. When she put her hand in his, a hand that held hearts from all over the country and always held hers, he pulled her into a hug.

"You don't need to worry about them. Your Gram did the right thing." Still holding her, he took a step back, "You and I, and Gram, know that those boys would have wasted the money in a hot minute, and your mother would be even more stuck up than she is now. I love her, but she can be, well, never mind that. Your Gram knew what she was doing, and it is a good thing." He leaned down to whisper in her ear, "I would recommend getting a better lawyer than this guy though, and a good investor. You're going to need it."

Her eyes shifted to Mr. Nettles to see if he heard, but the man was busy at his desk.

Her daddy kissed her cheek and left her standing in the middle of the dated office. There was no going back to her simple life. Gram had changed all that. What worried Beth was whether it was for the better.

Journal Entry
  May 13th
  What was she thinking by leaving me almost everything? My mother is clearly furious. My sisters are green with envy. My only ally is daddy.
  I'll do my best to fulfill her wishes, but it won't be easy. God, I need some help. They will shred me so they can get what they want. I need

to gather up all the courage I can to complete the task Gram has given me. Talk about being thrown into a lion's den.

 **Note to whoever reads this—if or when I go missing, talk to mother first.

Beth

*a*fter days of worry over what to do next, Beth decided to take a drive around the countryside. With the cover off of her 1970 soft top Ford Bronco, she welcomed the wind blowing through her hair. Cornfields fresh with new growth flashed in her periphery while the sun beat down on her head. Drives on a sunny day were usually what she needed to clear her head. It wasn't working this time though. The questions wouldn't stop flowing.

What am I supposed to do with all this money?

How do I keep my family from wanting to murder me?

Why would Gram make me her heir instead of Mother?

Completely irritated at the lack of answers, Beth found a place to pull over. A small farm sat to her right, while an open field of wildflowers swayed in the warm breeze to her left. As she cut the engine, a friendly goat approached the fence line and began to bleat at her. A long-haired cow followed and proceeded to moo. Their need to be heard brought a smile to her face.

The thick envelope Mr. Nettles handed her came to mind: *There is a letter inside with instructions from your grandmother.* It sat on the passenger side under her hobo bag, so Beth reached for it and pulled it a little too hard, dumping her bag on the floor of the Bronco. She ignored the mess as she fiddled with the clasp to open it. Her shaking fingers made it difficult to get a good grip.

"*Slow down, sugar.*" Gram's common phrase to her when she was too worked up clicked in her mind. Beth rested her hands and envelope in her lap, leaned her head back and closed her eyes. In through the nose, out through the mouth. In through the nose, out through the mouth. She did this several times until the shaking ceased. Beth lifted the packet back up and opened it with ease.

Inside, she found an envelope that she had seen several times on Gram's office desk. The smooth linen-cotton blend paper in soft white with Gram's initials embossed on the back was scented with the familiar Coco Channel scent. Beth pulled the tri-fold paper out of the envelope with reverence as she took in the jagged script of Gram's aging hand. An image of the beloved matriarch seated at her little desk in her padded chair constricted Beth's heart as the pain of loss spread through her chest.

My dearest Elizabeth,

I want to apologize for not warning you of my decision to make you heir instead of your mother. I can see her expression now and hear her shriek as I write this. How my daughter became the woman she did, I will never know. I don't recall spoiling her. Lord knows I disciplined her when needed and was firm with my rules, but for some reason, she became the woman you know. I am just sorry you have to face her alone. I can only pray that your daddy will keep her at bay.

Mr. Nettles will have told you about the house in Ann Arbor, but he left out one other piece of property. He did that per my request. In the stack of papers he gave you is the deed to the cottage on Merriweather Island. I know it has been some time since you were there last, but I am sure you still love it as much as I did. It held so many happy memories for us. It was the joy of our summers to have you spend time there with your granddad and me.

For years, Beth tried to get her parents to let her go back to the island after granddad's death, but reasons were always available as to why they couldn't.

So, here is what I would like you to do.

SELL and LEAVE THE STATE!

There is nothing here for you that will let you realize your dreams. Children must break free and spread their wings, or they will never find their own way. Sell everything in Michigan and take the money to live your life. Just keep the deed to the property on Merriweather Island. Move there if you would like. My request is that you hold on to the family property; you can only pass it on to your children. Promise me you will hold on to it.

"I promise, Gram."

My sweet girl, I just want you to know that I am so proud of you. You have made great strides to find your own way in this world, I can only hope that this money will help you to continue on. (You know, that food truck idea would be a great start. I heard the Independence Islands recently opened their doors to outside businesses, and your friend Mallory Barrows invited you there. Might be a great place to start. It's a thought.) Whatever you decide, pray about it first. God will guide your path, sugar.

I love you fifty bushels,

Gram

BAAAAAA! The goat startled her, causing the contents on her lap to spill to the floor.

"Well, BAAAA to you too," her foolish reply started a conversation with the goat by the fence. They "spoke" back and forth several times as she cleaned up the fallen papers before Beth let out a laugh and turned the key that brought life to her Bronco.

A weight had lifted from her shoulders. Though her heart was still heavy from the loss, she had direction. At least the first step. Sell the big house and the things inside. She pulled out

13

onto the road and made her way back to her little apartment downtown. Plans began to come to light as she navigated the streets.

Why wait to get started?

Beth pulled into the carpool parking lot off the highway and called her mother and sisters.

"Meet me at Gram's at six. I'm selling everything starting tomorrow. I would like you to get your things first."

All three began to argue but she cut it short by hanging up. She didn't want to be mean and inconsiderate, but she knew if she gave them any amount of her time, they would plant doubts or wear her down. She was invigorated and determined to carry out Gram's wishes and before the family ties that held her captive began to tighten the noose around her neck.

Today was her Independence Day.

Journal Entry

May 20th

Gram always told me that family was a gift from God so that we would never feel alone in this world. If that is the case, I think God hates me. Now, I know that isn't true, but the question has to be asked —why would He give me the kind of family I have? I should pray for grace or guidance. Frankly, I don't feel like it. Rather, I feel abandoned by Gram and God. I don't know how I will manage this enormous estate, though burning everything did come to mind the moment my mother and sisters started to fight, again.

I just don't know at this point.

Beth

4

*N*othing in the Stevens family ever happened in an easy manner, but Beth kept moving forward until freedom was in her grasp.

Her mother and sisters fought her every step of the way. *Keep the house, sell the house, keep the stuff, I hope you are donating all that money.* The backlash she received overwhelmed her at times, but then she would spot the letter and know that what she was doing was according to what Gram wanted. At least she hadn't needed to call the police to escort her mother from the premises.

Beth always knew that her mother could be irrational but what she had witnessed on a daily basis over the past two months was all the persuading she needed to move away. Her sisters used every excuse possible to explain away mother's behavior, "She's grieving. She did just lose her mother." She tried not to let it hurt, but the evenings of drowning her tears in Mackinaw Island Fudge ice cream only confirmed the pain.

The day she told her family that she was leaving town for good, a part of her hoped for some shed tears. Instead, she was met with a door in her face. She wanted to feel numb to the rejection, but the nagging pain lingered all the same.

When she went to her parents' spacious mansion to say good-bye, there was no one to be found even though she could hear her dad on the phone in his office and her mother screaming for the maid. Standing in the round foyer, she yelled "see ya later" one more time and walked out. Emotion clung to her throat as she made her way to her vehicle. Just as she reached for the door handle, the front door opened and shut with a bang. Startled, she watched her dad jog down the concrete steps to her. Engulfed in his warm embrace, she let the tears fall as he kissed her temple.

"I love you, baby girl. I hate seeing you leave, but I am proud of you for spreading your wings. You are setting out on your own path and walking away from the crazy expectations your mother had in mind for you." His words strained as a loan tear made a trail down his cheek.

Now, here she was, standing at the precipice of her future and it was all salty air and ocean breezes from here on out. Well, actually, it was the rail of the ferry that was taking her from her past and closer to independence. Independence Islands that is.

Beth rolled into Hilton Head, South Carolina to embark on the next phase of her life with a food truck trailer hitched to the back of the Bronco. The age of the early model SUV required a bit of a beef up to have the power to pull the trailer, but it was money well spent. She contemplated selling the Bronco and buying a half-ton truck, but the Bronco was her first vehicle, and the memories of Gram and her million-watt grin in the seat next to her made it hard to part with it. When the mechanic told her he could "increase the torque" she was on board with the plan.

Finding a trailer the size she needed to make it work and still tow well proved to be an entirely different challenge. It needed to be tall enough for one person to move in freely, wide enough to house all the cooking and refrigeration she needed, and still be light enough to not kill the transmission on the Bronco.

"Looks like the islands are getting another traveling business. I'm looking forward to sampling something different from clams, crabs, and fish." The low timbre of the husky voice beside her thundered in her chest and raised the hairs on her arms and neck. Beth looked to her right and caught a glimpse of the owner of such a commanding yet soothing voice. She took in the man's windblown brown locks that hung a little long on his collar. The lean, firm lines of his face were graced with a little more than a five o'clock shadow while his light green eyes, flecked with amber, froze all thought while accelerating her heart. The roguish upturn of his kissable, or rather well-shaped, mouth released a cluster of butterflies in her middle.

The man cleared his throat, forcing her to shake off the trance. Beth shifted her attention in several directions in an effort to avoid any more eye contact.

Say something, you twit.

"Has there ever been a food truck on the islands?"

"The main island, Mimosa Island, is the only one open to tourists. A little over six months ago, those living on the southern islands voted to allow some mobile businesses to travel the islands as a way to offer other resources. If this all works out, then the people will vote on what to do next."

"That explains why Mallory reached out to me. I knew about the 'no tourism' rule when I received her invitation. I'm glad I came down."

The man gave her a once over. "I'm glad you did, too."

The ferry gave a loud blast of the warning horn just as he was about to say something. Instead, he excused himself and left her side. She watched him as he walked away, a familiar sentiment Gram used to sputter ringing true for Beth for the first

17

time. "It's a shame he had to leave, but it sure is nice to watch him go."

Beth's cheeks warmed at the thought. "Nice one, Gram," she whispered to herself taking a little extra time to admire the man.

"He sure is fine," a woman declared from her left.

"Do you know him?" Beth asked, only giving the intruder a quick side glance.

"I only know of him. He is a staple around the islands. And someone I'm definitely hoping to get to know better."

There was something about the declaration that had Beth looking for a way out of the conversation. Maybe it was the woman's tone or the short shorts and low cut, spaghetti strap top. Turning her attention to the approaching dock, she excused herself and made her way to the Bronco.

Two more ferry rides, both shorter than the first, and Beth approached Pirates' Cove on Merriweather Island. The rocky cliffside jutted out from the rest of the island at the northern-most tip. A smaller lighthouse than the one across the water way on Breakers Head Island stood strong against the winds. Every so often, Beth caught a glint of reflection of the lantern room of the lighthouse. She took her phone out of her pocket to capture the image of Gram's cottage and the lighthouse in the same frame. When she prepared to share it with someone, Beth realized there was no one to share the image with. Her sisters wouldn't care, her mother wouldn't text, and her dad could be in surgery.

The once thatched roof of the cottage now sported a bright red, metal one. Stone walls gleamed white in the sun's light, igniting excitement within her. It had been such a long time since she had been to the island that she'd almost forgot how beautiful the site was. Now it was hers to care for.

Just beyond the cottage, spanning between Breakers Head and Merriweather Island, stood the first in a series of suspension bridges that connected the five southern islands, leaving out any connection to Mimosa except by ferry.

Merriweather Island's terrain reflected the shores of Northern Europe to the north, where her cottage was. The southern half of the island felt more like the sandy shores of Florida. As a girl, Beth would marvel at the change in scenery when she would ride her bike around the island. Pine trees and rocky hills in the mornings while sporting cable-knit sweaters and jeans. Then off to the beach in a bathing suit for the afternoon. Her summers never left her feeling bored but always felt shorter than they were.

One summer, Beth recalled, she sat under a blanket on the large yard swing, sandwiched between her grandparents. She couldn't have been more thirteen at the time. Her knees tucked up to her chest, she listened to granddad, the family storyteller, as he shared with her the island's origins and how it connected to her.

"You see, pumpkin, in the mid-seventeen hundreds, a privateer by the name of Sir Reginald Merriweather and his crew ran ashore on the east side of the island in a fierce storm. They found themselves stranded here for many months. While he and his crew explored the uncharted island in search of civilization and food, Sir Reginald wrote down all that he saw that day in a journal. He was marveled by the island's landscape, the diversity of the lush trees, and the richness of the soil. So he decided to lay claim to the island for his own and made it the crew's hideout. Some of the men established huts and traps while others repaired the ship. It was long before they could continue sailing on to the mainland and traversing up and down the coast.

"On one stop in Savannah, Sir Reginald met a lovely maiden by the name of Madeline. Her father was one of the founding British aristocrats to reside in the town. Her beauty beguiled him and yet he hid in the shadows to watch her coming and going."

Beth had stopped her granddad. "Isn't that a little creepy?"

"I'm sure it would look that way except it is said that he caught her eye just as much. They met secretly for only a few short weeks before Sir Reginald begged her to marry him and move to the island. She quickly agreed but was met with resistance from her father. She was about to marry a man who would only financially benefit the family, but rumors circulated that the man was gentler with horses than women. Her French mother made arrangements for their midnight nuptials, and the rest, as they say, is history. It took the love of a lady to make the privateer a family man, and it was their love that made Merriweather Island a home."

Now, the cottage that Reginald built for Madeline was hers. She could start her own legacy on the island.

"And here we are, folks. Welcome to Merriweather," the deep voice boomed through her thoughts.

"His voice is like warm honey," the woman from the ferry stated as Beth passed a little red Ferrari when the vessel approached the dock.

"Pardon me?"

"Don't you recognize the man? You spoke to him not two hours ago."

"That guy is the captain? I thought he was some local surfer or something."

"Oh no, that fine specimen is Scott Anderson. He's also the Independence Island's bachelor extraordinaire. A bit of a pirate in his own way. Stealing hearts from north to south." The woman's next sentence produced a crass statement and the provocative mannerism awakened a protectiveness in Beth for the man. She never felt the urge to hit someone, but if God saw fit to using Beth to slap the woman straight, she wouldn't argue.

The man's name, Scott Anderson, circled around in her mind.

I know that name, and those eyes were very familiar. How do I know...

A face formed from her memory. Young, ruddy features that smiled at her, begging her to follow him to some unknown destination. *It'll be fun. I promise we won't get in trouble.* Just like that, she knew exactly who he was.

For so many summers, she traipsed around the islands with Scott when she came down with Gram and Granddad. They met at camp the first summer and just continued to spend time together after the two-week camp ended. She could never decide if she was more excited to go to camp each year or spend time with her buddy Scott.

Her last summer, things changed.

Scott was going into his senior year of high school and the declining health of Beth's granddad left her uncertain if she would ever see him again. Their games were not as childish as in years past and Scott's behavior was more skittish. She asked him about it often, but he always deflected with a shoulder shrug.

One night, sitting on the sandy beaches of Merriweather Island, he did more than tell her what was on his mind. The sweet kiss that he branded her with left no room to wonder what was on his mind. Unfortunately, Granddad took a turn and her family left the island the next day. Their parting tore her heart apart. She dreamed of that kiss for nights on end, but it was the warmth of that last embrace that got her through the death of her granddad.

I could use one of those hugs now.

"The name is Valerie." The woman held out her well-manicured hand to Beth.

"I'm Elizabeth."

"So, where are you headed with that?" Valerie nodded toward her trailer.

"A business opportunity opened itself up and I am here to

see how things work out," Beth made a point to leave out details of her new residence.

"Well, I look forward to sampling your fare. What kind of food will you be sharing with the islanders?"

"Oh, a little of this, a little of that. Almost everything on the menu are recipes my Gram and I created."

The horn from the bow of the ferry announced their approach to the dock, giving Beth a way to escape the predatory woman. *Lord, keep Scott from her talons.*

Just as Beth climbed into the Bronco, the horn of the little red Ferrari blared, and Valerie's blood red fingers waved at her. Of course, the huntress possessed the flashiest car around. She plastered a smile on her face and waved back, cringing inside.

Beth crept off the ferry and onto dry ground, making sure to take in all the possible places she could park the truck in the cove, and at the same time, keeping an eye out for Scott.

The landscape of the island felt reminiscent of Michigan's own Mackinac Island. According to traffic signs, the main road that encircled the island was called Revolution Road. The road in front of her, connecting the East and West coasts, was called Captain's Walk. Sitting at the entrance to the Cove, the roads crossed before her. If she went straight, she would find herself in the heart of Reginald's Square. Almost like a belt around the middle of the island, the downtown area acted as the hub of all civilized activity, though it was rather limited. A little restaurant, a grocery store, and the church were all that consumed the Square. Beth made a mental note that she may have to start her own garden just to sustain her constant need for fresh vegetables.

Turning left on Revolution Road, she made her way to the cottage, her new home, and nothing could be sweeter. The wind fingered through her mahogany hair as she let the memories of her grandparents, summer camp, and Scott wash over her hurting soul.

As Beth came to the crest of the hill that acted as a barrier between the cottage and the rest of the world, the red roof top of her cottage welcomed her. She could only pray that she would find as much peace and joy within the protection of its walls as her grandparents did. And maybe even a little love on the beaches that hugged Merriweather Island.

Journal Entry
   August 20th
   I made it to Merriweather Island. I'd forgotten how beautiful and tranquil it is down here, but oh, the heat. I think my face melted on the ferry, but the occasional ocean spray helped.
   I ran into Scott Anderson, although he clearly didn't recognize me. I didn't think I had changed that much. Then again, I didn't know it was him I was talking to until that woman told me. I hope to see him again, soon.
   The cottage looks just like it used to apart from a few essential upgrades. It must have been fixed after Hurricane Irma. Gram told me it took a beating, but seeing the changes now, I realize we could have lost it all. Thank God for these heavy rock walls.
   I open business tomorrow. Wish me luck.
   Beth

"'ll handle it, Mayor. You have my word."

"You'd better, Scott. We don't need any outsiders cluttering up our island by squatting on land that isn't theirs."

Scott couldn't help but chuckle as images of the rotund, balding mayor, Chuck Ainsley, with a bright red face came to the forefront of his mind. Merriweather's illustrious mayor had a way of getting worked up over the littlest things.

A five-minute walk from his docked houseboat at the pier to his bicycle and a twenty-minute ride to the northernmost point of the island was all it would take to handle this emergency.

His thoughts wandered to the beauty he'd run into on the ferry the day before. There was something about her impish eyes that reminded him of a young girl he once knew. He was about to introduce himself to her, but the sound of the bell had spurred him into action. When he saw her on the ferry to Merriweather, he thought for sure he would be able to catch her.

As he approached the cottage, he caught sight of the food truck parked beside the cottage. Curiosity ignited energy into his legs, pushing him closer to discovering who the woman really was.

He parked his bike, unable to take his eyes off the monstrous contraption, and made his way to the front door of the cottage.

One knock produced silence.

Two knocks still offered no knowledge of the inhabitants.

The third try at least gave him a grumble and the crashing of pans, as well as his irritation overshadowing the hope of this being a quick stop.

"All right, whoever you are," he banged on the old wood door hard enough to rattle his own bones. "You need to move on. This is private property."

The door flung open to reveal a sleepy-eyed, brown haired beauty with a fire in her eyes. "No, Scott, you need to move. I own this property."

Scott watched her full lips turn upward, but not a sound was heard as his eyes traveled down to take in the woman's complete disarray. Instead of the put together woman from the ferries, he was greeted by a woman in a loose fit tank top that stated she was "Queen Bee" in sequins of black and gold. She paired it with shorts that could only be appropriate for in the house. He did his best to look away, but the amount of flesh that was on display would make any man's mouth dry.

He cleared his throat. "No, actually, this is private property, miss. Unless you have some legitimate reason to be here, I must ask you to get dressed and..." Then her words took hold in his head. "Wait, how do you know my name?"

Scott studied her face looking for something familiar. Something to invoke a memory or feeling. Then he caught it, that glimmer of stardust that radiated in her golden eyes. Only one other girl had eyes that color. A girl who kissed him goodbye and never looked back.

A war raged within him. A war between excitement to see an old friend and the hurt teenaged boy. The grin on her lips made the decision easy. He never could stay mad at her for long. That's when it hit him. If she was here, then where is...

"Is Gram here?" He asked a little too quickly.

Her features shifted to complete distress as her sleepy eyes turned to pools of anguish. Without a word, he had his answer, and his first love fell into his arms. He stood in her doorway in silence as she poured out her pain onto his shoulder. Her rushed words were difficult to understand at times, but he caught enough to know that a woman he admired was gone.

Elizabeth's bond with her Grandmother was undeniable. The elderly woman would tell him stories of their exploits in cooking and baking as well as how she was doing in her personal life. *"She still hasn't had a beau since her summers with you,"* the little matchmaker would write and tell him. Maybe they were closer than he imagined, maybe more like a mother than grandmother. He'd recalled seeing them sitting on the yard swing overlooking the Atlantic Ocean when he would come to visit in the evenings and the pain of loss radiated across his chest.

That was the one thing both of them had in common. One old woman loved them like their mothers should have. His mother was gone, passed on when he was a young boy. Her mother treated her like a second thought.

The crying began to recede, and Elizabeth backed out of his embrace, the breeze chilling the place on his chest where her cheek had rested. He wouldn't give attention to the fact that he kind of liked holding her, comforting her.

"I'm sorry about that, Scott." She did her best to wipe away the tear-soaked spots on his shirt, "I don't know what came over me. That probably wasn't how you expected to be greeted. I have been on autopilot." A piece of his heart broke for her as he watched her dab away her tears.

"It is definitely not what I expected but think nothing of it.

You clearly needed a shoulder. I'm sorry to hear about Gram. She was amazing. When did she …?"

"It was about three months ago."

He understood the feeling well. "Are you here to visit, then?"

"Actually, I am here to stay. I'm done with the cold weather and snow. She left me the property, encouraged me to get my business started, and Mallory Barrows invited me to bring my food truck to the islands. So, here I am."

Scott looked back to the mobile restaurant behind him. Instead of just painting an old camper, she had affixed wood slats to all four sides. At the top, a sign posted the name of the little eatery. *Comfort Cuisine.*

"What made you think of the name?" He asked.

Elizabeth didn't speak for a moment as the tears threatened to return. Scott clasped her hand and gave it a supportive squeeze as he waited.

"Every time I cook, I'm comforted by the fact that the recipes are diverse and created in love. I feel her with me with each dish that I make. The joy in creating well-made cuisine is what bonded us together, but it's the love that'll keep her with me forever."

Scott let her thoughtful response float around them as they surveyed the trailer. He knew the feeling. It was how he felt about the houseboat. He and his dad towed it to the islands when he was a kid and spent weeks working on it. It was their way of reconnecting after his mom died. Many times they took their frustrations out on the deck of the boat rather than one another. His father taught him about love, life, and faith as they completed each task.

"So, what brings you to my doorstep, Scott?" Her abrupt, almost accusatory tone caught him off guard.

"The mayor drove by and saw your set up. He thought you were a squatter or something. I take it you didn't report to the island office yet?"

"No, I didn't. I was overly tired and just wanted to get here. I'll stop there before I park. I have to show them my permit anyway," she cut her words short and to the point.

Scott looked at his watch, hiding the fact that her change in tone caught him off guard. "So, where do you plan to park this thing?"

"Wherever I am allowed but mostly in highly populated areas." She gave him a sideways glance. "Any recommendations, Scottie boy?" she asked as she bumped her shoulder into his arm and flashed a wink.

He couldn't help but chuckle at her question. "It really has been a long time since you were here last. There are very few 'highly populated areas.' You'll have to just watch and observe. I will say this, if you rise before the sun does, you can park near the docks or down by the beaches. There is no coffee house here. Only the mobile bookstore has coffee. I am sure that another truck with some coffee in the morning would be great."

"A mobile bookstore, huh? That's Mallory, isn't it?"

"That it is. You will only find her on this island on Tuesdays though. It is a tiny house on wheels. You can't miss it."

"I've known her almost as long as I've known you. I can't wait to see her again."

"You know, my appetite has increased now that I am a grown man. Want to give an old pal some hints as to what will be on the menu? I plan to be at that window every day."

"The menu will change each week. So, one never knows what is coming."

"I like that. If you cook as well as Gram, I am going to have to ride my bike more often," Scott began to rub his tummy as he walked away from her and toward his bike. He needed to make the next ferry departure. "I need to keep my girlish figure, you know?" Scott tossed a silly grin in Elizabeth's direction, giving him a glimpse of her pretty smile one more time.

"Good to see you again, Elizabeth," he waved goodbye while he hashed out ways to see her as often as possible.

"You too, Scott," she waved. "Oh, by the way, you can call me Beth. I know mom insisted you use my full name, but well, we're both adults now." He caught her meaning and agreed.

When Scott reached the ferry docks, he found the mayor there waiting for him, pacing back and forth along the length of the boat. He wrung his hands in an expectant, eager way. Something had the man jumping for more...of something. Who knew what the little man was cooking up, but it was never good when he looked the way he did. Like a man hatching a plan.

"*Scott!* My man! How did it go? Was the mission successful? Are they gone?"

"Well, no, at least not successful for you. I enjoyed the visit though. The person has a legal right to be there. You won't be running her out of there anytime soon." Scott eyed the man a little longer. "What does it matter to you anyway?"

"They have legal rights? What do you mean by that? No one has rights to that place except the old thorn in my side."

Perturbed beyond his normal limit now, Scott had a brief image of taking hold of the man by the collar of his shirt. Shaking the thoughts, he used his words instead. "You wouldn't be referring to Mrs. Merriweather-Lewis in such a way, would you? She's the reason you are even in this place, Chuck." Scott made sure to lace his voice with all the irritation he had burning in his chest. No one talked about Gram that way.

"Oh, Scott," the man did what he could to temper Scott's ire. He was failing miserably. Scott promised to serve the office, not the man. "You know how hard of a woman she was?" Scott only gave him a nod. Gram was stubborn, but she was always kind. "I was hoping she would leave the property to the island so we could turn that area into a real park. With it being a historical location and all."

"You know that will never happen, right?"

Chuck began to walk away, but as he turned, he mumbled, "I'll have to come up with another plan."

The whispered comment was just enough to bring everything within Scott to attention. It was never a good thing when a man like Charles Ainsley began scheming. People would get hurt and knowing Elizabeth could be at the end of that hurt did not sit well with Scott.

Journal Entry
August 21st

Man, Scott is cute and smells great too. What a way to be woken up first thing in the morning.

I slobbered all over him though. I'm not sure where that all came from, but I'll try to keep it together next time. Something about him made me feel safe enough to let a lot of emotions out. It's kind of scary. I came down here to find independence and the first thing I do is throw myself into some man's arms. I WON'T do that again. I need to be strong.

Beth

6

*B*eth was ready to throw in the towel. If one more thing went wrong, she might just pack up the trailer and go back to the cottage. Maybe even back to Michigan.

When she went to the mayor's office, the smarmy mayor seemed to have no issue with holding her back from making the lunch rush at the docks. Instead of glancing over the papers for the right signatures and looking to see what she would be selling, he made four phone calls, and read each document—word for word. One would think that the man would know what the document said. He then made snide comments about the necessity of her business, and how he believed only "citizens of the island should be allowed to live and work on his island." Adding to the insult of his rude behavior, he made sure to toss in chauvinistic remarks about women in the workplace. That was when Beth almost punched the guy in the nose, but that would be assault on a government official and she could kiss her dreams goodbye.

After enduring two hours of verbal abuse and sharing eye rolls with his sweet-tempered secretary, she had to drive over to the health inspector. The man had to inspect every aspect of her trailer before she could go set up at the docks. That event took another hour, but she expected it. The fact that the inspector was friendly and a bit chatty helped alleviate the anger and frustration the mayor caused.

She only had half an hour until lunch when she arrived at the dock, and it would take an hour to set up and warm up the cooktop. She shaved some of her time by not putting out her cafe tables and other signage. When she opened the window, she was met with fifteen hungry men. Scott stood in the forefront with a cheesy grin on his face and a boyish sparkle in his eyes. Her heart dropped and her mind began to change the menu for the day. Her original plan wasn't going to work.

"Good thing I baked and prepped the meatloaf," she spoke into the metal void of the trailer. She turned her back to the crowd, acting busier than what the meal called for, while making sure to bang a few pans and utensils together harder than necessary. Her nerves were on high alert and stalling just a bit gave her time to take a breath. When she felt she could no longer wait, she turned to meet the hungry crowd.

"Welcome, gentlemen. I want to thank you for being patient. Today's special is a meatloaf sandwich with chips, and a drink. I also have…"

"Oh, come on, lady. We're hungry, and our boss is cruel," a man yelled from the back. A collective chuckle rushed to her in a wave.

"Don't listen to Harry," Scott stated louder than necessary, looking over his shoulder so everyone could hear him. "He's always crabby. His boss thinks he is overpaid anyway." He leaned in and informed her that he was the boss. The rest of the group burst into laughter as the banter continued and a calming wave washed over her.

Scott turned his green eyes back to her. "The meatloaf is Gram's?"

"Well, part of it. The other part is mine."

"We will take fifteen meatloaf sandwich specials. I'm paying so they can eat what I tell them. Besides, I get the feeling it would be easier on you right now."

Scott gave her a wink before he turned to the guys, and she started slicing the meatloaf so that her flush was hidden. He always could turn her heart into a puddle. She couldn't think about that now, though. Her food truck and getting on her feet was all that mattered.

The click of the side door gave her a start, causing her to drop the knife that she was using on the counter. She looked to see who intruded, only to find Scott grabbing a frilly apron off the hook and placing a hair net on his head. Jabs and cat calls came from his employees as he crossed into their view.

"What on earth are you doing?"

"You need help, and they look hungry. Besides, this helps you focus on the sandwiches. I'll give the chips and sodas out. Teamwork makes the dream work, right?"

Not having time to argue, she pointed him to the proper cabinets and refrigerator and let him hand things out.

Placing the inch-thick meatloaf slices on the cooktop made a heavenly scent of the meat and spices fill the air. She caught a hint of moans and groans from those waiting and the gesture of pleasure brought a smile to her face. "Just wait until you bite into it, guys," Scott declared.

Standing in front of the food refrigerator looking for the cheese, it hit her that some of the guys may have an intolerance. Beth turned to Scott, "Any dairy allergies?" Scott shrugged and turned to the guys. He asked, and they replied with a resounding "NO!"

She placed slices of gouda cheese on each piece of meatloaf, letting the heat turn the soft cheese into a gooey mess. Next, she set ciabatta bun halves inside facing down on the buttery cooktop on so the bread could toast while she prepped the mushroom, onion, garlic mixture.

Music from her phone began to play over the Bluetooth speaker system in the trailer. The intro of Lauren Daigle's latest song release connected with Beth's muscle memory and she moved to the rhythm of the peppy tune as she chopped, flipped, and built the sandwiches. She moved about the small space in tandem with Scott, never once bumping into each other. She handed him perfectly wrapped sandwiches, sealed with her signature sticker label while he placed them in the tray with the chips and a pickle and distributed the meals to his crew. Working with someone in a kitchen brought her a sense of peace.

After she handed Scott the last sandwich, she turned to see where he was at in distributing the meals. The sight of him smiling as he joked with his crew opened a small window into her heart, shining a light on the fondness they once shared. Their natural ability to work together so well in such a tight space only softened her heart toward him. *Not part of the plan right now, Beth.*

Scott handed the workers their sandwiches with a smile and a "You're welcome". Service and generosity poured from him as he gave each worker his undivided attention. He cared about each person and it showed. Who wouldn't want to have a guy like that as a boss? What girl wouldn't want a guy like that to come home to? *Elizabeth! I said not yet!*

"Earth to Elizabeth," Beth blinked to see Scott waving a hand in her face. "Are you okay?"

"Just watching the patrons enjoy their food." Yup, she lied. She wasn't about to tell him the truth.

"Well, our lunch break is over. Do you think you can handle it from here?" His eyes teased her while he removed the frilly apron.

And then a switch flipped inside her.

Does he think I'm incapable of doing this? He's just like Mom. Well, I'll show him.

"Yeah, I can handle this just fine. It isn't like I asked you to jump in here and be my knight in, in…frilly apron. I could have managed." The adrenaline that surged through her veins pumped like a raging river, but it was the change in his expression that indicated that she had taken things too far.

Scott hung up the apron, threw his hands up, and left the trailer without a word. He just left.

Her eyes followed the swagger of his walk as he made his way to the ferry dock. With every step he made away from her, another click of regret over her behavior pricked her heart. *Girl, you are a mess. Yesterday, you threw yourself in his arms, slobbering all over him like a Saint Bernard. Today, you treat him like an intruder when he helps you out in the middle of your first lunch rush. You better get yourself together.*

"Hey, is this the kind of service we can expect, lady?" A gruff sailor scolded from the window.

"Sorry," she grabbed her point of sale system while shaking off her bad behavior. "What can I get you, sir?"

He gave her his order, *Fish taco with fries and a coke.* She excused herself and began to prepare the order.

Making the meal was as simple as making the fifteen meatloaf sandwiches. The convictions in her heart consumed her thoughts as she moved about in the kitchen alone. What had made her so irrational? It had never been an issue before. In fact, she was the levelheaded one in her family, not giving in to emotional swings.

"Here you go, sir. Thank you for your patience." She handed the meal to the man, and he took a seat on a nearby bench.

Beth turned to pack away the food, clean the cooktop, and wipe down the stainless-steel counters all while trying to not think about what she'd done. Maybe she could push it to the back of her mind, and it would eventually go away.

"You look like you're a woman lost. Well, lost in thought." Beth turned to see who had approached in such a stealthy manner only to find Mallory Barrows on the other side of the window.

"Yeah, just a little. It has been a crazy day," she glanced at her clock on the wall. "Wow, it's two. It's later than I thought."

"Island time can creep up on you. How are you settling in?"

"Come on in for a chat. I'll make you something to eat. Or I have pie if you prefer. Whichever you like." A friend was exactly what she needed right now.

"How about that peach pie I see you advertising on your signboard? With a little whipped cream on top." Compassion radiated off her.

Beth went to work preparing the pie, taking a few more steps than necessary to hide from the kindness that Mallory's brown eyes offered her. There had only been one other person with eyes like that. What she wouldn't give to share all this with Gram.

"So, how are you? It has been a long time since we've seen you around here."

Beth contemplated her answer as she served Mallory her pie. How much should she share? The basics wouldn't hurt.

"Gram left me an inheritance that included the cottage on the north point overlooking Pirates' Cove and the bridge."

"That was generous of her. That property has been in the family since this island was first discovered."

"That is what she told me," Beth sat on the bench seat across from Mallory. The memory of the many times Gram had shared the story brought a smile to her face. "I can't believe she's gone, Mallory," the recent ache began to grow. "How am I going to do this without her? She was my rock. My ally when things were crazy. Who do I turn to now?"

Mallory assessed Beth in silent contemplation. Beth could see her friend carefully processing her thoughts to better offer her advice.

"What happened to your faith, Bett—erm, Beth?" Mallory's

natural tendency to refer to Beth by an old nickname tripped her up, but she knew immediately what Mallory was saying.

A pain in her chest muted her, and a nod was all she offered in reply.

"Okay, so take the pain and crazy thoughts to God," Mallory's brilliant smile softened the hard truth of her words. "You can also count on your friends. I'm only a phone call away, and if we happen to be on the same island, I can check in on you or you can stop by The Book Barrow." She tilted her head and shot a cheeky grin Beth's way. "Or there is that hunky ferry boat captain slash resident fisherman, Scott Anderson, who I am sure would like to pick up where things left off."

"I can't call on him. He makes me feel ..." Beth searched for the right word, but Mallory beat her to it.

"He makes you feel, period."

"What he makes me feel is angry. He's condescending and chauvinistic."

"I'm sorry, are we talking about the same Scott Anderson? That sounds nothing like him. The lady doth protest too much, methinks."

Beth couldn't hold in the laughter at Mallory's quirky voice as she spoke.

"He always has been a bit of a nice pirate, hasn't he?" Beth remarked as a younger version of the man came to mind. His once long locks blowing in the salty breeze as he emerged from the ocean in only swim trunks with a surfboard under his arm. He stole her heart that summer — like a pirate stole treasure from the kings of Europe, and he made no apologies.

"I take it your family did not react well to your Grandmother's choice to leave you so much."

"Not at all. I've never fit in my family. A non-conformist or rebel-child, so to speak. My mother is a lot like Mrs. Bennet from Pride and Prejudice. My sisters were compliant to her demands to marry young and have lots of children. I dug in my heels, and she hates it." Beth looked down to her hands that rested on the table and began picking at her fingers. "When I left Michigan, only my dad saw me off."

Mallory moved from her side of the table to scoot in beside Beth, wrapping an arm around her shoulders. "If you are doing exactly what God has shown you to do, then don't worry about what your family thinks. You are here for a reason. Don't lose sight of that."

Tears sprang to Beth's eyes as Mallory's words soaked into her soul, pouring over her heart like warm honey. God had a reason for bringing her to Merriweather Island. The least she could do is seek Him out to discover the reason why.

Journal Entry

August 21ˢᵗ pt 2

1) Scott is still hot in the heat of the day and a bit of a saint, even when I'm crazy.

2) Thank God for sending Mallory back into my life

3) The Mayor is a weasel that must be avoided at all costs.

4) I am beat. Good night!

Beth

7

*S*cott watched over Beth from afar for a week, looking for an opportunity to speak with her about their last encounter. Somehow, he had offended her, and he needed to clear the air. Seven nights of broken sleep because of the incident was pushing him to the edge of his sanity. Never being one to like having a bad feeling hanging over his head, he typically tried to resolve issues quickly. His crazy tour boat schedule and Beth's avoidance of him on the streets had made it impossible to make things right. Today, that would end.

Not wanting bad feelings between them was not the only reason Scott wanted to clear things up. There was something about her that drew his daily thoughts to her. Many of his memories of her were from their younger days, but the grown-up version of her was even more appealing. Her sincere smile and rapt attention to each person captivated him. From the comments of the guys working the docks, he wasn't the only one. *"I'd go back just to see her smile. The food is a bonus treat. Don't tell my Sally that I prefer a food truck's Reuben over hers."*

"If you keep watching her like that, passersby will think

you're lovesick, Cap," his first mate, Thaddeus, stated with a chuckle.

"I'm not watching her. You just caught me looking in that direction."

"Yeah, for a little longer than is necessary. Why don't you go talk to her again? You two worked well together that day. Like she lived here as long as you had and the two of you were the best of friends. If not more," Thaddeus winked.

"Can it, Thad. She has enough on her hands. Besides, we were kids last time she was in town."

"I'm just sayin' is all. Have a good lunch, boss," the man waved as he walked away.

Thaddeus had a point though. Here Scott sat, every afternoon, admiring her from the same picnic table at the same time. *When did you become a chicken, Scotty?*

Determination to resolve things with Beth pushed him to his feet, tossing his half-eaten sandwich to the pelican that had been eyeing him for the last twenty minutes. If he didn't move now, he may not later. A subtle recollection of two heartsick teens kissing on the beach over on Hooper Island floated through his mind while strawberry bubblegum had left its sticky sweet flavor on her lips. It had done dangerous things to his younger self, things that he didn't know how to handle at the time. Since her return, he wondered if she still used the same flavor lip balm. *Don't go there, Scott.*

"Ouch!" The feminine cry for help stopped Scott in his tracks. Being the next best thing to a first responder, he knew he had to perform a duty, even though he would rather talk to Beth.

Searching the park for the injured woman, Scott soon discovered who required his help, and it was not someone he wanted to deal with. Valerie sat in the grass, rubbing her ankle while giving him the occasional glance. He'd never had the pleasure to meet the red-haired siren, but he heard plenty of tales.

According to the guys, she'd set her sights on him, but that only made him want to hide out on the mainland.

"Oh, Lord, do I have to?" He knew the answer, but it didn't mean he would enjoy the encounter.

Longing to prolong a delay in the meeting, Scott made his way to Beth and her Comfort Cuisine food trailer. He'd do the right thing and bring her a bag of ice for her ankle. It would also give him an opening to bridge the gap between him and Beth.

"Good afternoon, Beth."

"Good afternoon. What can I get for you? Fish tacos are the special today."

"That sounds amazing, but what I need right now," he gestured with his thumb in the direction of the fallen woman, "is a sandwich bag full of ice. Do you have some to spare?"

Beth looked in the direction he indicated, then back to him. She gave him an understanding nod before she filled his request. When she came back to the window, she had more than the ice bag for him. "Here's some water as well. It's getting warm. And when you are finished, I'll have a couple of fish tacos ready for you."

Her peace gesture in the form of one of his favorite lunches was the olive branch he needed. He lifted the bottle, "Thank you. I'll be back."

He walked only a few feet when Beth called out to him. "Watch yourself, Scotty boy. She has eyes on you."

Scott nodded and turned to help.

He trod across the park, his feet felt heavy like they were encased in cement, forcing his stride to seem slower than what it was. When he was only a mere five steps away, she began her theatrics. "Oh, I think I broke it. I can't believe I was so silly."

Her voluptuous red lips winced with pain, but it never reached the rest of her features. He doubted how severe she was truly hurt. *Be slow to judge.* He'd find out soon enough.

"Here comes my hero. And with ice and water. You do think

of everything." Her red polished nails glimmered in the sun's rays. The way she moved her hands toward him gave an unsubtle hint that she required his help rising from the grass. He refrained from lifting her up from the grass. Fake injury or not, he had to be sure before he helped her stand.

"Actually, Beth thought you would appreciate the water. I just brought some ice." Scott knelt beside her and examine her ankle.

"I'm Scott, by the way."

"Oh, I know, well at least I have heard, in passing. Anyway, I'm Valerie." She held out her hand to him and he quickly shook it.

Valerie opened the bottled water and lifted it to her full red lips. After taking a brief drink, she put the cap back in place and then put the ice-cold bottle to the side her neck, "Oh, that is cold, and very refreshing. Thank you, kind knight." As she moved the dripping bottle from one side of her neck to the other, Scott got the clear signal of where she was trying to draw his attention. The discomfort from her behavior only pushed him to put more distance between them.

Upon close inspection of the ankle, he discovered that there was no break or even swelling to hint at a sprain. He would play along with her charade for now. When he pressed his fingers in different areas around her ankle and foot and noted that she never once winced or ceased talking, he rose and held out a hand to her.

He wouldn't call her out on her fib with so many people around, but he was not going to waste any more time. "There is no break from what I can see, but I can help you to a bench. I am sure that once you are off your foot for a bit, you will be just fine."

Scott turned to find a bench that rested under a tree. Only ten steps away and he would be free.

If he didn't feel like a piece of meat every time she looked at him, then maybe he would be more of a southern gentleman. If this is the way some women felt when men looked them up and down or worse, then it was no wonder they were crying "foul" on every news outlet and media source these days.

Putting one arm around her waist, he supported Valerie while carrying her purse and the water.

"Thank you so much for your kindness. Not many are so caring."

He could hear her desire for some sort of attention in her voice. *I'll help her, Lord, but not sure I can befriend her. Give her someone to show her how valuable she is to You.*

"It's not a problem, ma'am." He helped her get situated in the shade, making sure her foot rested on the seat of the bench with ice on her ankle. "I think you will be just fine. Rest a bit and you will be fine in no time. But don't sit out here too much longer. It's gonna be a scorcher."

Valerie gave her thanks again as he turned and walked back to the safety of *Comfort Cuisine*. Guilt at not doing more tried to creep in and haunt him but seeing the radiant smile on Beth's face was enough to wipe it away. To appease his nagging conscience, he placed a call into the central dispatch and told them about Valerie's situation.

He approached Comfort Cuisine, "I'm here for my hero's reward." He made sure to sport the biggest, cheesiest grin he could muster. The one that always made Beth laugh when they were younger.

She didn't disappoint in her response to his goofy behavior. Her melodious laughter wrapped around his heart and squeezed. "You have earned it, gallant knight."

Scott held out his hands to accept the mouthwatering reward. "I thank you, milady." His laughter joined hers, calling attention to their antics. "Do you have time to come out here and sit at one of your tables with me?"

Her hesitance became painfully obvious, but she covered it

as quickly as possible. "Don't you have to get back to your ferry? And haven't you had your lunch?"

"Probably should and some pelican ate my sandwich." He still wanted to talk to her though. "Are you available tonight? I'd like to talk and catch up with you."

Journal Entry

August 27ᵗʰ

Scott is coming by tonight. I know I promised myself I would keep my distance, but I need a friend. Why does it have to be a guy I used to have a thing for? His kindness today with that woman, Valerie, looked a little painful. She pawed at him like a needy puppy. I did notice other women giving him a flirty look or two as well. All the more reason to keep our relationship in the friend zone. I need to curb the attraction and just be a friend.

I hope I can do it.

Beth

8

"What am I doing?" Beth asked herself as she towel dried and scrunched her hair to give it some volume and beach waves. She was taking too much care in getting ready to see Scott. "Just friends" became her mantra as she continued preening.

She'd seen the hope in his eyes the second she'd agreed to his request, but now she regretted it. It didn't take a genius to figure out why he wanted to come by. After she lashed out at him for helping, she was so ashamed by her behavior that she avoided him as much as possible.

Throughout the week, she would catch him looking her way as she served customers. At times, he was stoic and hard to read. Then there were those moments when she thought he had something to say until he turned around and walked away.

A knock on the door pulled him from her thoughts. "Here we go."

Grabbing her lightweight cardigan off the foot of the bed, Beth descended the stairs and to the front door. *He's just a friend. It's not a date.* She could see the top of his head through the arched windows on the door. His swaying left to right and back again spoke of his nerves at the looming encounter. She couldn't help but smile when she thought of his shifting habit when he was unsure about something. When she was young, she thought it was cute and endearing.

Beth squeezed the doorknob a little harder than usual, pausing for a breath before she opened the solid oak door. "Hi," was all that would come out of her mouth.

"Hi to you, too," Scott gave her a sideways grin that deepened the dimples he tried his best to hide with his day-old beard.

"Come on in," Beth stepped aside to give him space. The entrance to the tiny cottage was hardly enough room for one person, let alone two. "I have to get the pork out of the oven for tomorrow's lunch before we go."

"Wow, do you ever not cook?" He joked as he walked through the door. He took a deep breath, his eyes closed and smile deepened. "Then again, if I produced food as tempting as you do, I might cook all the time as well."

Beth turned away to hide the blush that she could feel heating her cheeks. "Well, as long as there are people to feed, I must provide. Besides, I have to make my way over to Mimosa for a Food Truck Rally they are having. I want to provide all of my best dishes and my Cuban pulled pork is one of them. It is a great way to get my name out there."

They entered the kitchen that Gram had updated at some point to look a little less rustic than it once did. Cupboard doors replaced the blue and white gingham fabric that hid the pots and pans. The floating shelves where still in place but the Formica counter tops were replaced with butcher-block. The new feature in the kitchen was a long, narrow island that ran parallel to the counter. It had been topped in stainless steel, which was perfect for prepping for the food truck.

"Hey, the kitchen looks great," Scott's tone sounded a little over done and it made her wonder if he didn't already know about it.

"Yeah, she never told me she was having it fixed up."

"Well, she didn't have a choice. After Irma, the whole inside needed a facelift. I spent enough time in here before, so I knew what to do to restore it, but she had some things she wanted changed."

"Wait, you did all this? Scott, this is beautiful."

"Well, I am glad you like it."

Beth moved to the oven where mitts waited for her to pull the pork roast from the oven.

"So, are you serving your fish tacos as well? It would be a shame if you didn't offer those."

"I am. I'll prep that onsite though. We both know what rewarmed fish can do to your internal reflexes." Both shivered and gave a mock gag in remembrance of the bad fish sandwiches they had in high school. "It took me years to eat fish again."

"I hadn't eaten the stuff again until I saw it on your menu. I trust your cooking skills."

Beth placed a hand over her heart, batted her eyes, and gave an exaggerated Southern accent laden reply, "Why, thank you, kind sir."

The more they talked, the lighter she began to feel. Scott wouldn't be standing in her kitchen with that adorably eager smile on his face. Maybe things weren't as bad as she imagined.

Once she pulled the pork from the oven, Beth proceeded to brush more of her homemade brown-sugar barbecue sauce over the meat. Moans of delight came from her left as Scott inched closer to get a better look and smell. She could feel him lean into her shoulder. He inhaled and released a breath, which grazed the hairs on the side of her head, sending shivers down her spine. "Heavenly," he mumbled.

Beth stepped away to gain her bearing. She looked back at

him and teased, "If you drool on my meat, I will hurt you, Anderson."

"Just a nibble?" Her salivating friend offered her the saddest case of puppy dog eyes she'd ever witnessed.

"How do I resist that face?" She took a knife out of the drawer and cut a small slice, the pork falling apart under the pressure. *Perfection.*

Not wanting him to touch any of the meat, she placed the piece on a small plate, removed the gloves she put on before brushing the sauce on the meat, and handed him the plate. His excitement over the morsel filled her with happiness. He placed a piece of meat in his mouth and his eyes shut in pure bliss. It was a struggle not to stare at the glazing of sauce left on his lips, looking just as delicious as the hunk of meat on the platter in front of her. *Whoa, girl!*

"Oh, that is too good." Scott went in for another bite, then another but when his piece was gone, he moved to sneak another piece from the pan.

"If you continue to eat my product, I will have to charge you double for all the profits I would lose." Beth couldn't help but laugh at his pout.

"I suppose you're right. I'll help you wrap this back up and then we can go for a walk. I'd like to catch up."

The hopefulness in his eyes as they went about the kitchen softened her resolve to remain indifferent to him. They'd been too close of friends before to avoid him now. Beth gave in and went through the door he opened for her.

Once outside, the late summer winds swirled around her as she stood in awe of the beauty of early sunset. The lights on the bridge connecting to Breakers Head were just beginning to flicker on. She relished the sound of the crashing waves below until a hand pressed on the small of her back, sending pinpricks of awareness up her spine.

"It never gets old, does it?" Scott's tone captured the reverence of the sight.

"No, it doesn't. At least I hope it never does. When I was here last, I was only starting to appreciate the beauty of this place," she looked to see if his face reflected the recollection of the moment she was referring to. The signature "Scott" grin gave her the answer.

"Let's walk," he swung his arm out to show her the direction he wanted to go. Fantastic. There would be a constant view of the bridge and the setting sun for at least half the walk.

They made small talk for a few paces but soon transitioned into catching up on island happenings.

There is no future with a pastor's son. He is not the kind of boy your dad and I have in mind for you. You're never coming back here again; do you understand me? Beth was horrified at her mother's words. Not that it was a surprise. It wasn't, but, when Beth turned to run away, Scott stood within earshot of them. She never could get the lost look he had on his face out of her mind. She told Gram she would never return strictly because of her mother's behavior.

Thank you, Gram, for making me come back. You knew I would need a friend.

"Penny for your thoughts?" Scott's whispered near her ear, causing another wave of tingles down her arms.

"Thinking about Gram. Thanking her for making me come back here."

"That woman had a way of making a person do things you didn't want to, but somehow she knew you needed to. Man, to have that ability must be amazing."

"She called it a 'God-given gift' of wisdom and discernment that is only given when asked for. I haven't asked God for anything, let alone special gifts like that, in years. Lately it has been more like, 'God, keep me from messing up.'"

"Why is that?" Scott took her hand and stopped their walk.

She turned to him and the seriousness in his eyes sent off alarms inside. "You were always on top of your daily time with God. You knew things that baffled me, and I'm a PK. What's going on in that head of yours? Why did you stop?"

She searched her memory for a recent time she prayed fervently about something. Only one moment came to mind.

"The day of Gram's will reading I gave a little halfhearted one, but there was no 'calling an angel down on my behalf.' It was more like, 'Okay God, if you say so.'"

Scott began to walk again, and she followed. "When was the last time before that?"

Her irritation at his prying questions began to rise. Copping an attitude came easy. "What does it matter to you? I don't know. And I'm not really sure I care. Why would I wanna take time to talk to a God who would give me such a messed-up family?"

Scott raised his hands in surrender and did his best to douse the angry flame that was beginning to burn in her. "I'm not passing judgment on you. I'm just asking a thoughtful question, like I used to. Remember our talks on this cliff? We would challenge each other, kind of an 'iron sharpens iron' thing. Talking things out always helped us process. You seem to have some things you need to process. I mean, let's face it, your behavior since you arrived has been a little weird as far as you and I are concerned." He cupped her hand in his, running his thumb across her knuckles, "Talk to me, Beth."

Guilt washed over her has she reached for Scott's hand. "I'm sorry. You're right. I've been crazy lately and I'm not sure why. I could give all the excuses in the world, but none of it will make sense."

"You're probably still grieving. I know I went through the same thing when Dad died. When someone as special as Gram, or Dad, is no longer with us, it is bound to have an effect on a person. If you need to talk though, you know I'm here, right?

I'm sure Mallory would too. We have all lost someone special in recent months, we could help each other."

"She and I have already talked a little bit. You're right, though. I could use all the help I can get right now. I came here to discover my place in the world, to figure out who I am, to do something I can be proud of. Not hide away like a hermit."

They began making their way back towards the cottage, the stars twinkling from above with the dark sky as the backdrop.

"So, you know I'm here for you and only want to help you, right?"

"Yes, Scott, I do know that. Thank you for being patient with me. I'll try not to bite the helping hand anymore."

"Good. So, do you need extra help tomorrow? I am available." Scott's grin made it difficult for her not to laugh.

"Only if you can keep your fingers out of the pork and not eat all my fish tacos."

Scott held up two fingers and placed his right hand over his heart, "You have my word."

"Okay, you're hired."

Lord, help me not to be crazy tomorrow.

Journal Entry
   August 27th pt. 2
   I'm going to be in a tiny space with Scott all day tomorrow. I'm not sure this will be a good thing.
   Beth

9

*L*ike a well-oiled machine, they worked in tandem serving the tourists of Mimosa Island for its Food Truck Throw Down. Scott never thought it was necessary to attend one of the events, but now he wished he had. There were food trucks from all over the south, and some from the New England area, teasing his senses with their sweet and savory aromas.

"How can you come to these and not eat your weight in food that might be very bad for you? I think I walked by a truck that was serving funnel cakes only. I walked by another that served all vegan and gluten free options. I'd be as big as a house."

"I don't smell it, Scott. All I smell is what I am making. The trick is to never walk the strip. Why do you think that back closet is a little bathroom? Besides, I can't leave the truck."

"I think you're full of it, and you slowly die a little with every gust of air that carries the aromas to you," Scott teased as a familiar patron approached the window.

"Well, lookie here. I take it you two worked things out?" Thaddeus laughed.

"We have reached a truce, but don't let on that you and I

chatted about it. She's pretty private about stuff," Scott whispered back.

Thaddeus gave a wink and ordered the pulled pork sandwich.

"Extra sauce? Slaw or Mac and Cheese? Soda or sweet tea?" Scott looked back to Beth for her approval that he did it right.

"No to the extra sauce. I like to taste the meat. Yes to the slaw and the Mac. I want to see if this Yankee girl knows how to make them right," Thaddeus laughed at his own joke. "Oh, and how could you ask a proper Southern boy if he wanted anything other than a sweet tea? Sheesh man, I think you're hanging out with her too much."

"Maybe that's a good thing," Beth said from the griddle behind him. She came around to the window with Thaddeus' mini tray of food. "Enjoy your meal, sir."

Scott tried not to laugh when she gave the old codger a wink and a curtsy. He sure had missed her wit and spunk. "I look forward to hearing what you think. I hope you enjoy."

The hours continued to pass, the sun began to set on the horizon, and the crowd never once died down. They ran out of a few things—certain kinds of beverages and condiments—but Beth's efficiency kept the food flowing at a steady pace.

When Scott noticed people walking past, not just the *Comfort Cuisine* but every food truck, he stopped working in auto pilot and observed the festival again. He looked to see where Beth was, only to find her cleaning the grill and countertops. "Is that it?" He blinked, caught off guard by the abrupt ending. "Now we just pack up and leave?" Scott hoped he didn't sound as desperate as he felt. He'd hoped to stay a little longer and enjoy the event.

"Well, we can beat the traffic and head back now. Or we can stay and go to the dance. Every vendor donated something to a VIP booth so that the vendors can sample each other's food."

53

"So, there is more! Well, let's stay. Have some fun. I think we both worked hard enough to deserve it."

She gave him a knowing smile that lit a fire in his heart. "Let me go clean up real quick." She tossed a rag at him. "Make sure *all* the surfaces are clean and close the window. I'll meet you out front in ten minutes."

She tossed him a look before she disappeared into the back room that he always thought was another closet. It only fanned the flame that began to burn. He went to work and moved fast, if only to recover from her flirting.

He waited out in front of the trailer, doing his best to ignore the surge of feelings within him as he watched people walk by.

Groups of college students passed, laughing at one thing or another. A few were clearly intoxicated, and Scott could only pray that they safely reached their hotels.

There were quite a few family groups as well. Moms, dads, some with older children, many with toddlers and babies in strollers. One of the older toddlers must have recognized him when his parents stopped at *Comfort Cuisine* around lunch time because Scott caught him bouncing in his daddy's arms, pointing in his direction. He waved at the boy.

A couple passed, hand in hand, as they strolled toward the dance hall. Adoration shown in their eyes as the glanced at each other. Scott couldn't help but follow them with his gaze as the guy brought their clutched hands up and he placed a kiss on her knuckles. The pureness of the moment shed a light on a longing he had buried deep. *I want that, Lord. Someone who looks at me with such love. Someone I can hold and protect like that.*

The squeak of the hinges on the trailer door broke his concentration on the couple. He turned to find Beth closing the door, and his mouth went dry. She hadn't just freshened up. She'd changed her clothes and hair completely. Maybe even showered. *How did she do that?*

Though the hem and necklines were modest, the coral

sundress hugged her curves in just the right places. He couldn't help but do a once-over on her just to take in all the changes she had made in just ten minutes. Her feet were even looking light and unhindered in the strapped sandals she had on.

"You ready?" she called to him.

"How did, when did you," *form a complete sentence, man,* ".... Wow, Beth. You clean up quick, and you look amazing. How did you manage that?"

"Magic!" She gave him an over-exaggerated hand gesture in the air and teased him with a look. Her laughter twisted a knot in his stomach.

Laughing with her, he offered her his elbow, praying she would take it. When she put her hand though it, he thought he would fly right out of his shoes. *Slow and steady, Scott. It's only been a couple months.* "You can tell me as we make our way to the VIP tent and dance hall."

"Don't you know, a lady never reveals her secrets?" They laughed.

"It used to be a midsized camper, so I just had them leave all the plumbing there but update it. This way, if I have had a long day in front of the grill, like today, then I can clean up."

Doing his best to be a gentleman, Scott struggled to keep his thoughts in the moment and not let his testosterone gorged mind wander.

"Well, at least you are prepared. Did you have to do anything special since you handle food on the trailer?"

Beth went on to explain the process to him, but he only caught half of what she said. He was too enthralled with how nice her hand felt on his arm. But a small voice in the back of his heart screamed at him to slow down—not to be so quick to give away his heart.

When he loved someone, it was all or nothing. He virtually removed his heart from his chest and placed it in the woman's hands. The positive to it, as his mother once told him, was that it showed his dedication to one person at any cost. It also displayed his willingness to trust easily. The open hole it left, though, was never filled to capacity each time a woman threw it back into his chest.

Maybe it's just that you gave it away to the girl on your arm so many years ago, and you have only been offering a fake heart to all the other girls since.

Something about the thought rang true. He did give her his real heart, the whole thing. Because she never knew she had it, she never gave it back and he never asked for it back.

"Scott, are you okay? Did you hear me?"

Oops.

"I'm sorry, Beth. My mind was wandering. What did you ask?"

She nailed him with a disbelieving look but let it pass. "I asked if you wanted to eat or dance first."

That was a difficult question at the moment. His body demanded sustenance, but he wanted to hold her longer. *Play it cool.* "Let's eat first. I'm pretty hungry. My boss was relentless today and worked me like a pack mule." He couldn't help but laugh at her bewildered expression, and it was just the thing to break the tension building in him so that they could enjoy the rest of the evening.

They laughed and teased during mini food fights and even shared each other's drinks, reminding him of how fun it was to be together. They were once quite the pair of rabble-rousers, island hopping to see what goofy thing they could do next. He was pretty sure that if cell phones had the capabilities then that they do now, their foolishness would have been documented and might have gotten them in jail for a night.

He took hold of Beth's hand and tugged her toward the dance hall. "Wanna know what I'm thinking about right now?"

"I'm afraid to ask, but let me have it."

"Remember the day we took the ferry to Savannah, seeing

the sights that we'd seen a dozen times before, but that time we made up our own stories for them?'

"I do. I think that was the time we stalked one particular tour guide and told him he was wrong about pieces of information he was giving the tourists. I think that is why they make them take classes now."

They both laughed at the memory.

"Do you remember what we did to the Waving Girl Statue?" Scott gave Beth a pointed look and wiggled his eyebrows in a Groucho Marx fashion.

"Oh, I wish I didn't."

"I wondered how long it took them to discover her." Beth raised her hands and made air quotes, "'Dress up clothes?'"

"You mean her tricorn hat, eye patch, and her dog's bandana? It didn't take them long, I'm sure."

It took them twelve hours exactly. Scott recalled being woken in an abrupt manner by his furious dad. Two officers saw them on a surveillance camera and knew where to find him. They'd made him do volunteer work for three months around Savannah and the islands. He would never tell her that.

The dance hall glistened in the soft glow of the twinkle lights hanging from open rafters. The cover band played a nineties country tune that Scott remembered well and stirred more romantic memories to surface.

"Wanna dance?" He asked as he gestured at the dance floor.

She looked from his eyes to the people dancing and back to him. "Sure."

Just as they were in place on the dance floor, they changed to an old Joe Cocker tune. One that made him think of her frequently. They swayed in sync with each other and the music. He watched her as she did her best not to meet his gaze. Part of him wanted her to look his way, the other was glad she didn't. Kissing her would be more tempting, and it was clear they had a long way to go before that. He had to do something though to get his mind off her lips.

"Today was fun. Thank you for asking to come along."

That got her attention. Her reply was slow coming but eventually she spoke. "It was nice to have you with me. To have a friend in the hole with me that I can trust."

"Tonight has been fun as well. I've missed you." The moment he said the words, he wanted to take them back. Not because he didn't mean them, but the look of fear in her eyes stabbed him in the heart. "I'm sorry, Beth. I…"

"No, it's okay. I missed you, too. You were a good friend, and the fact that we could pick right back up like we hadn't spent the last ten years apart is comforting. Gram told me to come down here and reconnect, and I didn't. I wish I had. All my real friends live on the islands. Down here, friends are family. Not because of genetics, but because of choice." The smile on her face and the mistiness of her eyes drove her message straight to his heart.

"Then welcome home, Beth."

Journal Entry

August 29ᵗʰ

I stressed the "friends only" thing last night, but boy was it hard not to lean in a little closer when we danced or to send a few flirty smiles his way.

He is so easy to read. His face tells me what is on his mind. Like when I came out of the trailer in the sundress or when I told him I was glad to have such a good friend in him. His face was hopeful before the dance and stricken after. I hate doing this to him, but I need time.

I don't want to depend on anyone. I have this freedom to come and go as I please without mother or some other person telling me I can't. I believe that is why Gram gave me the inheritance. I was lost in everyone else's version of me. Not mine or God's, but all the outside forces. Even Scott, no matter how sweet he is, sees me as the teenaged version of myself. That girl is long gone, and I don't know how to make him see.

Oh well, it will come to me, eventually.

Beth

*B*eth locked up her food truck a few minutes early, excitement for the rest of the day coursing through her veins. The birds darted back and forth over head, diving into the water at various intervals. Two weeks had passed since the Food Truck Throw Down, and her attraction to Scott left her confused and angry with herself. Today, she would not think about him. She'd been looking forward to this meeting with some old friends since Mallory called to tell her about it.

Taking a little stroll up Captain's Walk to Madeline Lane to clear her head, Beth took time to take in the "downtown" area. It wasn't like a conventional urban area like back home. It was more of a smattering of colonial homes turned into small businesses that sat on each side of Madeline Lane to Reginald Square, and very sporadic at that. There was no order or thought to the placement of each home. Like the house was just dropped and left. No formal rows of brick buildings either. The only brick structure was the municipal building near the docks.

At the end of the lane, up on a hill, sat the main church. Its stark white clapboard siding amplified the light and shined down the hill onto the little town. Halfway down the hill, to the south of the church, sat a large home. It was once the parsonage. Apparently, the pastors who came to Merriweather had large families. Its trendy Nordic look indicated that it had been updated.

Just past the church, Banner's General Store sat. Beth had visited there a few times already, and it was nice having them on the island when she was in a pinch and ran out of something. The store carried just enough of the basics to feed and clothe the few hundred residences of Merriweather.

If an outsider came to the island and saw how scarce the buildings were, they would think it a ghost town. Locals knew that the homes and buildings still standing were the ones that survived the frequent hurricanes that came through. Why these lasted so long, God only knew. Yet they stood strong, like a beacon, displaying their builder's pride in the craftsmanship to withstand the occasional one hundred mile per hour winds.

It was Granny Mae's Cafe that Beth was looking for though. The only diner on the whole island served the locals daily. It was open until six most days and closed long enough for Sunday services before opening back up after church for the lunch crowd. It was also the reason why Beth traveled to the other islands on varying days of the week. Giving an established business competition was not her goal in coming. She'd only serve Merriweather on Mondays.

Climbing the front steps of the wraparound porch that graced the cafe, Beth gave a quick scan through the windows to see if she could see her friends. Samantha, Kendall, Melody, Penelope, Mallory and Beth first met when Beth was ten, at a church camp on Skye Island. That first year, they all slept in the same bunkhouse and solidified their friendship over late-night storytelling and pillow fights. When they parted ways their last year together, they promised to remain pen pals.

Inside, Beth was transported back in time by the classic traditional elements of floral wallpaper, thick oak wood trim, and hardwood oak floors. The high ceilings gave the rooms a larger-than-life feel. The smells coming from the kitchen teased Beth's senses, drawing her in with savory aromas like sage, rosemary, and garlic.

"Good afternoon, sugar. I'm Granny Mae. You here alone or to meet someone? If you're alone, I have a couple of good-looking, smart young men at the bar in the back for ya..."

Beth raised her hand to stop the sweet, nosy elderly woman. "I'm here to meet some friends."

"Well, good!" The woman's voice carried through the room. "You must be part of the group I saw in the parlor. Come with me, darlin'. Now, if'n you change your mind, I'll introduce you to the boys later." The woman offered a wink. If the woman hadn't been so cute, Beth might have gotten irritated with the meddling.

"There she is! Late as always."

Beth searched the room for the owner of the voice and found a round table full of women, all standing to greet her. Mallory met her halfway across the room, wrapping her in a hug. The endearing action was unusual for her friend, but Beth went with it. "You are far from late," she whispered. "They just arrived early."

"Hey, you can't hog her all to yourself, Mallory. Bring her on over here," ordered Penelope. She was always prepared, hyper-organized, and bubbly-to-boot.

"Look at you. You haven't aged at all. It's just not fair," Melody declared as she wrapped Beth in her warm embrace. The auburn beauty had no issues with saying what was on her mind, but her sweetness always showed through. "Unlike some of us," she stated as she turned back to the table.

"Well, it's been over ten years since we were last together. What do you expect?" Pen joked as she passed a glance in Beth and Mallory's direction.

"I don't look old, do I?" Mallory asked Beth under her breath.

"No, you look beautiful."

A red-headed beauty rose from her chair and wrapped Beth in her arms, "It's so good to see you again, Beth. I've missed you." If Beth couldn't already tell from the hair that it was Kendall Mulligan, it would have been the warmth of her hug. She was one of the friendliest people Beth had ever met.

Next to embrace her was Samantha with her bleach blond, California waves, perfectly toned tan, and the only one who was the same height as Beth. "It's good to see you, girl."

"It's good to be seen."

"Well, let's get this luncheon started," Melody chimed in after she wrapped her arms around Beth.

Everyone at the table lightly groaned but quickly followed with a round of laughs as the six of them reminisced about their days at camp. Especially at all the gags they played on Melody since she was the baby of the group.

"That Nair prank was the best though." Samantha laughed.

"It was not," Melody defensiveness flared like it had happened last week. "My mom went into a full-blown panic attack over the bald spot on my head when I got home that year. I wore a ponytail for almost a year before I had enough growth to sport a cute bob."

Kendall asked whose idea it'd been in the first place. Beth took that moment to play with her salad knowing full well who came up with it. Pen caught Beth's shiftiness and called her out.

"Beeeth?" A snicker followed, "It was you, wasn't it?"

"Can I plead the fifth?"

"Only in a court of law, Beth. You were always the mastermind behind the pranks. I bet you were behind the one I heard about that happened in Savannah," Mallory's pointing finger waving at Beth while she did her best not to laugh.

"When was that one?"

"I never heard about that."

"What happened?"

"I heard someone put a tricorn hat and an eye patch on the Waving Girl statue and a bandana on the head of the dog beside her. It didn't take them long to find a suspect, but Beth was never implicated."

"Mallory, I haven't the foggiest idea what you're talking about," Beth chuckled.

"You may not, but it sounds like something you would do." The rest of the women at the table agreed. Beth just shrugged her shoulders and refused to confirm or deny.

"Speaking of pranks and camp, I heard they were remodeling the cabins this year. The camp received a large donation making it possible to finally make the repairs," Samantha announced.

"That's great news."

"That had to cost a pretty penny."

"Who did it?" Kendall asked.

Beth knew the answer, but she wasn't about to make an announcement. *When you give to the poor, don't let your left hand know what your right hand is doing.* It wasn't anyone's business who donated the money, anyway. Having been blessed by her inheritance, there was no reason she couldn't put the money to good use. The place made an impact on her life, and scores of others needed help. The choice was easy.

"It was an anonymous donor, I guess," Samantha answered. "They called Greener Gardens to do an estimate for some landscaping. I might donate time or materials. As a former camper, it's the least I can do."

"Do you think they would take help from other campers? Maybe I can persuade them to have a big reopening," Pen began to lay out a plan for "the party of the year" to celebrate and a way to get more of the past kids to help with the work.

Mallory chimed in, "Let's first find out if they need or want help. Then we can plan."

They all agreed, and they moved on to things like business and men. Beth really didn't feel like divulging those areas of her life, so she made attempts to change the subject. It didn't go according to plan, so she used the one tactic she learned from her family - avoidance. She listened to their conversations while picking through her salad. If she didn't make eye contact with anyone, they wouldn't pull her in.

"Well, hello there, ladies."

That familiar bass made her heart accelerate and the bite she just swallowed began to turn in her stomach. She didn't have to look up at him to know that he stood close to her. He placed his hand on the back of her chair, his fingers skimming her back. The simple touch, probably unintentional, sent tingles down her spine. With every word spoken to others at the table, the scent of peppermint-tinted breath made its way down to her, brushing the side of her neck. Memories of dancing under the fairy lights assaulted her, making it hard to focus on anything else besides how close he stood.

"Hi, Beth."

She took a sip of water to give herself a couple more heart beats to pull things together. "Hi, Scott," she said as she turned to face him. No need to be rude to someone who did so much to help her. "Are you rested from Saturday?" she asked him.

"I am. It was fun. Thaddeus is still talking about your barbecue. He was telling all the guys to order it with the mac and cheese. He wasn't too impressed with the coleslaw though."

"Well, it is not the most popular side dish. That also explains the recent interest in that sandwich."

"Yeah, it would," Scott knelt down so that they would meet each other's eyes. "It's called job security, too."

He placed his hand on her bare arm, sending slivers of electricity straight to her toes. "Are you okay, Beth?" He asked in a more private tone. "You look a little peaked."

"I'm fine. Thank you," she offered her most lady like smile. If only he would quit touching her maybe she wouldn't look so flushed.

"Okay," he stood back up and said his goodbyes to the rest of the table.

And then it began.

"What was that?"

"Someone has it bad."

"I don't think I have ever seen you that red."

"Please tell me you are going to say yes. I want to plan your wedding."

Oh, I don't think so!

"It was nothing and will never be something. We are friends, and that is how it will stay. And Pen, you can plan someone else's wedding but not mine." Beth made a point to look each one of her well-intentioned friends in the eyes as she spoke. "Now, can we talk about something else?"

Journal Entry

September 19ᵗʰ

Girlfriends. Oh, how I have missed having girlfriends. Friends to laugh about silly things with and tell secrets to. It has been so long since I had other women around me that are my age and understand the struggles in love, work, and faith.

I hope I didn't come off too harsh when Pen asked to plan my wedding to Scott. Marriage to anyone is the furthest thing from my mind right now, but when people see two people of opposite genders act in a way that is teasing or caring, they seem to assume it means more. Maybe it will, someday, and maybe it won't. Let's not push it.

Beth

"*M*r. Ainsley will be out in just a moment, Scott."

"Thank you, Sarah."

Scott turned to have a seat in the makeshift seating area, but the recent changes did not go unnoticed. When they had converted an old Victorian parsonage that sat on the hill near the church into the mayor's mansion, the dining room had been converted to a receiving area while the parlor had been converted to the mayor's office. They'd called him to head the remodel, but he refused to ruin the character of the house. Judging by the clean, monochromatic color scheme and the missing oak trim and hardwood floors, Mayor Ainsley had found someone else to do the job.

The grandfather clock in the hall clicked the seconds away, and its rhythm highlighted the tapping of Sarah's fingers on the keys of her computer.

"Mayor Ainsley's office, this is Sarah. How may I help you today?"

Scott listened to her handle the call, and there was something in her voice that hinted at her recent heartbreak. Life on a small collection of islands wasn't much different from any other small town. News traveled fast when the story was scandalous, worthy of celebration, or tragic. The Reid family's story fit the latter.

Once she hung up the phone, Scott approached her desk. "So, how are things with you and the kids? I haven't had a chance to say hello the last few times I stopped to see Chuck."

"Oh, it is sweet of you to ask. Davy, Tommy, and I are doing well enough. Thankfully, David set things up to have the loans all paid if something ever happened to him. I just received a notice for the last loan payoff."

The forming sheen in her eyes tugged on his own emotions. It had only been six months since David's death and the loss of his friend was still fresh. He couldn't imagine losing a spouse.

"He looked out for you. That's all any man could hope to do," Scott reached in his back pocket, pulled out his wallet and extracted a business card. "If you need anything around the house, please feel free to call me."

Sarah's face fell in a puddle of relief and heartache as she hurried around the desk and wrapped Scott in her arms. "Thank you so much. I didn't want to ask, but..."

Her words muffled as she buried her face in his shirt. When her words came out a little more stuttered, Scott pushed her back and gazed at her. "Sarah, I can help, but I need you to settle down a bit."

"Sarah! Send him in!" Charles Ainsley's voice boomed in a condescending manner from his office and Scott's anger toward the man began to boil. Sarah's response to his simple offer indicated to him that she wasn't doing well, and that man was screaming at her from across the house.

Why are grieving women throwing themselves at me? And Lord, help me to not throttle that man when I go in there.

Scott waited until Sarah was settled before he let her go. He ignored the fool hollering for her. If the man stormed from his office to scold her, Scott had no problem defending her.

"I'm good now, Scott. Thank you."

"I'll call you tonight. I may have to have a buddy come help, but we will get this taken care of."

Fresh tears began to travel down her face. "Thank you."

Scott stomped to the office door, the fire in his veins consuming his thoughts. Men like their infamous mayor were the worst of the worst, and he was ready to let the mayor know it.

Be slow to speak, quick to listen.

The reprimand doused the flame by the time he reached the door. He was behaving irrationally and needed to pause before he entered the room.

He took a deep breath as he took hold of the doorknob. "Give me peace."

"Ah, finally! You're not out there fraternizing with my help, are you, Scott?"

The comment only irked him more.

"No more than you are bothering to show a widow a little kindness right now."

The dumbfounded look on Charles' face spoke about the man's lack of understanding. *How did he ever become mayor?*

"No, Chuck. I wasn't fraternizing with Mrs. Reid. Now, what did you summon me here for? I have work to do."

"Yes, I did call. Have a seat, my boy, we need to make a game plan."

Scott hesitated, sitting in the leather high back chair across from Charles. He didn't have time for three hours to listen to the man's ramblings. "What plan is that?"

"Are you daft, man? Why, how we are going to get Miss Stevens out of that cottage, of course. Where is your head at, Scott?"

Now it was time for Scott to look dumbfounded. "I have no intention of helping you force her out. She has been through enough in the last six months. She needs a haven right now."

Scott pushed himself back up on his feet. "I'm not going to take part in criminal activity either, Chuck. I know you forced out the Williams sisters from this place to further your agenda. I don't know how you got away with it, but I won't watch that happen again."

Charles stood from his chair, the vein on the side of his neck beginning to pulse. "I thought you would do whatever I needed, Scott. I need you to help me with this."

Scott's hands fisted while that small voice inside reminded him to *be slow to anger*, even if it was justifiable. Resting his fisted hands on the desk, he leaned in. "I will help 'serve and protect.' I will not destroy."

Scott clenched and unclenched his fist as his ability to control his actions lessened. If he stayed in the presence of the grimy, manipulative, and shady behavior of the man, he might just do something that would get him in trouble with the law. Scott stormed for the door and flung it open, letting it hit the wall of the office without a care to the damage it may cause.

Scott waved good-bye to Sarah as he passed her desk. He could hear the concern in her voice when she said, "Bye," but at this point his only focus was to get as far from that man as possible.

The rage that built within him burned white hot and he knew being around people would not be a good idea right now. Scott's steps pounded into the ground as he walked out his anger. Folks may have spoken to him, but he wouldn't know. For that matter, he had no idea where he'd go even. But if he didn't get away—very far away—things could go bad. *God, why do you let people like Charles Ainsley become leaders?*

When Scott finally looked up to see where he was, he saw the North bridge peeking over the hill. Judging the distance from the mayor's mansion to the bridge, Scott figured he had been walking for an hour. He hadn't prayed—only grumbled and raged over the encounter. When more of the bridge came into view, guilt over losing his temper began to wash over him.

How could I lose it so quickly?

"You are a protector, my dear son. It is just how God made you," his mother once told him after he came home from school bruised and battered from a fight. A friend of his had been bullied by another student. When things turned to verbal blows, the things that were said to his friend made Scott so mad that it sparked angry tears. Before he knew what happened, he had sent a left hook to the kid's jaw.

That was precisely what Scott longed to do to Charles Ainsley, but he couldn't. That may have been just a school yard fight back then, but now it would be considered assault and battery.

"Father, help me fight the anger and desire to react. Show me how to walk in Your ways and not my own."

"Amen," a soft voice agreed. Scott knew who it belonged to without having to turn to see her beside him.

"Amen."

"I didn't hear you approach. How long have we been walking together?" Beth's stride matched his step for step. Her slow, easy smile offered him a lifeline. He wasn't alone.

"Oh, long enough to see you storm from the mayor's mansion and almost to my doorstep. Which is right over the ridge, by the way."

Scott stopped and finally took a minute to take in his surroundings. The tall grasses of the hillside blew in the warm sea breeze while gulls flew overhead. He didn't even recall crossing over the road coming off the bridge to walk the paths to her house. "So, the whole way is what you're saying? What are you, a stalker?" he teased.

Beth offered a soft chuckle, but then her expression grew somber. "I have only seen that level of rage in you one other time. It was terrifying when you defended me all those years ago as a child and it was pretty terrifying this time. I just prayed while you stormed on."

What man wouldn't want a woman like Elizabeth Stevens in his corner? Scott put an arm around Beth's shoulders and pulled her to his side. As they began to walk again, Beth slid her arm around his waist. "Thank you, Beth."

"For what?"

Scott searched for the right words to use without scaring her or saying something he wasn't ready to declare yet. "For being you." *Be my wife?* The sudden thought caused Scott's heart to skip a beat, but he refused to give in to its affects, so he kept hold of her and continued walking.

Beth's silence rattled him. She always replied in humble tones when she was complimented. He could only hope he didn't say that last bit aloud.

When the bright red door of the cottage became more visible, and Beth still had not spoken after their stroll, Scott glanced down at her. What he saw startled him enough to stop him in his tracks. She stopped as well but didn't turn to face him.

He turned her to face him, gently lifted her chin with his finger, and wiped the tears that streamed down her face with his thumb as he cupped her cheek. "Your eyes are leaking, Ferret."

The use of the childhood nickname produced the response he was hoping for. Laughter.

"Why did you start calling me that?" she sputtered.

"During one of our pranks, I think it was when we T.P.'d the sheriff's house, I saw you weave between branches in the big oak tree in the yard and thought of a ferret. I mean, you were long-legged, had a lean frame and a ponytail that was long and bushy like a ferret tail. Then when they yelled at us out of their window, you squeaked like one. I couldn't help it."

"But they are so stinky."

"Not when their owner takes care of them." Again, there was

more he wanted to say but wouldn't. "So, are you going to tell me why you were crying?"

He waited for her while she avoided his gaze and picked at the button on his pocket. His heart pounded on his chest so hard that he was sure she could see it.

"It was what you said."

Worry crept up to his throat and threatened to choke him. He had to have said the words out loud.

"What did I say? Did I offend you, hurt you?" Her continued silence began to twist him in knots. "Please tell me so I can..."

"It was the nicest thing anyone has ever said to me, and I mean ever, Scott. No one in my life, besides Gram of course."

Her pain sent fresh tears coursing down her face, and he fought hard not to kiss every single one of them away.

"No one has told you what an amazing woman you are?"

She only shook her head.

Scott didn't say another word but pulled her to him and held her until the sobbing stopped.

God, help me to show her how special she is and somehow reveal to her how You see her. Oh, and help me not mess this up. I can't watch her leave again.

Journal Entry

September 28th

I tried to be supportive, but I ended up broken in his arms, again. Will I ever be normal again? Will the pain ever go away? Will I ever see myself the way he sees me? The way Gram saw me?

I am broken, lying here in pieces, waiting for someone to put me back together. I can't do it on my own, I need help.

Beth

*C*harles Ainsley observed Valerie from a few feet away. She looked to be pouting as she watched the thorn in his side, Scott. The woman followed the man around like a lost puppy looking for some sign that her owner loved her. Scott's refusal to help told Charles that the man's affections were clearly taken with that short-order cook.

From what he heard and saw of Valerie, he knew she would do anything to get the man's attention. Desperation oozed from her flaming red lips. If she was needing attention, she sure had it. His. He would use it to get what he wanted, and maybe he could get her what she wanted. A win-win plan because it would get rid of Elizabeth Stevens.

Slithering in her direction, Charles almost floated to the woman's side despite his portly girth. The closer he got, the more he knew that she was just the pawn he needed to carry out his devilish plan. Sloped shoulders, mascara streaked face, puppy dog eyes—all perfect indicators of a desperate woman.

"Why, Miss Hornigold," Charles knew when to lay on the charm, and this situation called for a thick coating. "You look like you have lost your best pair of Louis Vuitton's. Whatever is the matter?"

The woman sniffed as she attempted to pull herself together. "Oh, nothing, Mr. Ainsley, thank you for asking. At least nothing for you to worry about. You have more important things to do than fuss over me."

"Oh, child, of course not. If there is something I can do to better serve one of my fellow constituents, I surely must do my best to hear them out. It's only Christian."

He did his best to keep his irritation from showing on his face when the woman still would not answer him and proceeded to blow her nose. When the hiccups began, he pulled the "concerned parent" routine out of his bag of people management tricks.

He put an arm around Valerie's shoulders and shushed as the blubbering increased. "It's all right, darlin'. You just let it out. Then you can tell Uncle Chuck all about it."

"It's just…I like him so much. Now that Stevens woman is here…oh, he doesn't even see me…Everything I dreamed of my life is dying." She sniffled again. "It's that stupid woman's fault. I wish she would just go away."

There was his window.

"Oh, now, Scott is an upstanding guy. I am sure he is just being nice."

"He sniffs around her and that food truck like a hungry bear. It's infuriating and heartbreaking at the same time. I should just forget him…but I can't," the last bit brought a fresh wave of tears.

Her carrying-on was beginning to get on his nerves, so he pushed a little more. "Listen, if you want him that bad, why not help him purge himself of his little temptation?"

Sniff. "What?"

"Show him why you're the better choice. I saw your performance with the ankle bit, now kick it up a notch. Pour on that sweet southern charm and show him why you're the girl for him. Once he chooses you, she'll leave."

"Really? I've never thought of that."

Of course you didn't.

"Oh, women do it all the time."

"Well, I'm not sure. I don't think he would even notice. She's won him over with her cooking. He hasn't been seen around the islands with anyone else but her since she arrived."

"I have a surefire plan to make it happen. Would you like to help me? It will be the perfect way to get back at the woman who wronged you and reignite an old family feud between the Hornigolds and the Merriweathers."

The sniffles and blubbering ceased, the tears stilled, and the color returned to Valerie's face. He had her attention.

There would be nothing better to run the food truck cook out than to pour a little gasoline on the embers of a centuries old feud between the descendants of Captain Merriweather and Captain Hornigold.

"Tell me."

And now he had her commitment. This would be too easy.

"Well, why don't you meet me in my office in a half an hour? I'll tell you the plan."

Valerie stuck out her hand, he took it and she shook in agreement. "I'll see you soon, Mr. Ainsley."

They both stood. "I look forward to it. Now go clean yourself up a bit. We want him to see why you are the better choice."

Valerie agreed and scurried off down the sidewalk. Charles took a few extra seconds to enjoy the view of her walking away before he turned to complete the task that brought him to the cove to begin with.

All sweetness pushed aside, he zeroed in on Scott who was tying up his boat for the night. Now that he definitely no longer needed the man's services, he had some choice words to say.

"Anderson!" He barked from half a dock away. "I've got a few words to say to you."

Scott turned. "Good for you! You can do all the talking you want, but I won't be replying."

Charles reached into his inside breast pocket and removed an envelope. "That works just fine for me. Your voice now grates on my nerves. I'm about to have a meeting, and I don't need your voice ringing in my ears."

Scott stopped what he was doing and gave Charles a look that set his temper on fire. "How in the world did you ever get elected? That is the most childish..."

Shutting the man up, Charles slapped the envelope into Scott's chest. "You promised you wouldn't talk. Consider yourself no longer employed by the state of Georgia and the mayor's office. You made a huge mistake turning me down for that little outsider. You and she will live to regret it."

Charles turned to walk away, imagining the dumbfounded look on Scott's face. Maybe he would even do a little groveling as well, but all he would do is kick him in the chops when he came back to him. He had a new lackey, and Scott's services were no longer required.

13

*S*cott would have kissed her if she'd given him the go-ahead, and that's why she had avoided him the next three days. He didn't indicate that he was thinking about it, but she saw it in his eyes, and it terrified her. She wanted to enjoy the rekindled friendship—the laughter, the talks, the mischief. Letting the friendship become more would only ruin things.

"Lord, I need a friend, not an emotional entanglement. I don't even know what tomorrow holds," Beth muttered as she leaned on the counter of her food truck while she watched the kids play in the park of Hooper Island. The moms sat at the picnic tables on one side watching their young ones and laughing together. They all had something in common that bound them together in friendship. Beth had one person like that. Gram.

She warned you to go make friends, and you never listened.

"What has you looking all dreamy?" Valerie's nasally voice broke through her pondering.

"Just thinking. What can I get for you?"

"Oh nothin'. I just saw you over here and I thought I would say howdy." She placed her perfectly manicured hand on the counter and began tapping her fingers. Visions of pulling the retractable window down on her hand danced in her head but she shook it away. Gram would start chasing her with a switch. The visual of eighty-year-old Gram running brought a smile to her face, changing her mood.

"Are you waiting for someone? Would you like a water while you wait?"

Valerie stood by the window, her profile only visible to Beth. Complete disgust for those walking by was evident on her face. The longer the woman waited to answer Beth's question, the higher her irritation level rose.

"Oh, I don't see him," she spoke as if to herself but loud enough for Beth to hear. She finally turned to Beth, "Do you have sparkling water? Maybe with some flavor?"

"I have cans of sparkling water that are berry infused, or I have filtered bottled water."

The woman's sneer was almost enough to tempt Beth to vault over the counter and shove the bottle down her—

"Oh, just give me the can." She pulled out her wallet to retrieve her money mumbling how uncivilized she was for not carrying...

Blah, blah, blah.

Beth quit listening and turned to get the drink, hoping the woman would leave soon.

Why do you let her get under your skin, darlin? Gram's voice scolded.

Why did she? Beth handed Valerie the can and took her money. Then she leaned back against the counter, crossed her arms and watched the primped princess drink the beverage.

Beth searched for the reason she didn't like the woman. *Is it her style? Her makeup is heavy? No, that's too petty.*

Valerie shifted her stance that was abrupt enough to make Beth take notice. She put the can down and began to smooth out her skintight fuchsia dress, and lastly, she fluffed her hair.

Beth tried hard not to laugh at the efforts the woman was going to so that someone would notice her. She caught sight of Scott strutting down the sidewalk with that smile she loved spread across his face. That's when a light went off—she didn't like the woman because Valerie had her eyes set on Scott. Her Scott.

He isn't yours though. Remember, you don't want him for anything more than a friend.

When he finally looked at the Comfort Cuisine, Scott's steps slowed. His face was making it obvious that he was not looking forward to the encounter as much as Beth was unwilling to witness it.

"Hello, ladies," Scott nodded to acknowledge them.

Valerie stepped closer to Scott while he seemed to struggle to stay rooted in his place. "Hello, Scott. I was just about to order something, but I was waiting for a customer to ask what they would recommend. I don't really trust food trucks, you know. One just never knows how long the food has been in the heat."

While the woman blatantly insulted Beth and her business, in front of her no less, Scott was quick to come to her defense.

"Now Valerie, you and I both know she has to follow strict rules. I love her food and have never gotten sick."

There was something about the way Valerie touched and fawned over Scott that called to the angry tigress in her. Beth had no real claim on the man, but a part of her still ached to protect what her heart felt was hers.

"Well, what do you recommend, Scott?" Valerie asked in such a simpering way that Beth thought she might be sick.

"Um," he took a second to clear his throat and stepped back. "Let's ask what the menu is today." His eyes shifted to Beth and pleaded for help. "Beth, what've you got for us today?"

Her menu consisted of some of the messiest handheld foods from home. Scott would love it all, Valerie might not.

"I have Coney dogs, chili dogs, sloppy Joes, half pound

cheeseburgers, and freshly made corn dogs. All come with fries, chips, or coleslaw for a side and a drink."

A smile spread on Scott's face while Valerie's confusion and horror were evident. "What is a Coney dog?" she sputtered. Scott knew and seemed to be drooling at the thought.

"It is a hot dog, nestled in a warm bun with a bean-less chili meat sauce poured over it. You can add white onions, mustard, and cheese if you like."

"Oh, you know me. I'll take two Coney's. If that is on the menu, why are you not busier?"

Beth went ahead and made the order. "I have no idea. I have it on several signs throughout the park and around the trailer. I guess everyone around here ate on Mimosa."

"Is it your grandma's recipe? Please tell me it is," Scott's pleading made Beth forget about the other night and the third wheel next to him. He could be hilarious when he tried.

"It sure is, with an added kick. I won't tell you what," Beth dipped a plastic spoon in the sauce to offer him a sample. "But see if you can guess."

Beth did not miss the look of disgust on Valerie's face as the spoon passed through the window. Scott's face on the other hand displayed total pleasure.

She finished his order while he rattled off guesses, never coming close to the truth.

"What is it Beth? It's amazing."

"You know, I think I'll keep it to myself. Secret recipe," she gave him a wink not even thinking about how he might take it.

"You're a cruel woman, but okay," he took his order and made his way to the nearby bistro tables she traveled with for patrons to sit at.

"How about you? What would you like?" Beth turned to Valerie, and she thought the woman would lose the lunch she hadn't even eaten yet.

"I'll just drink my water. I'm vegan, and you've got a slaughterhouse for a menu. You two should be ashamed of yourselves. Your blatant disregard for animal life is appalling." She turned to Scott, "And I thought I knew you."

"I have a strawberry, spinach, and feta cheese salad," Beth offered.

"Yuck, that is just as bad. I'll never eat here."

Valerie did an about face and stormed down the hill, struggling to walk in the grass with her mile-high stilettos. Beth had to remind herself that it wouldn't be nice to laugh.

That's when something dropped from the sky as a seagull passed. Beth and Scott stared in total disbelief, then looked back to each other.

"Did that—"

"Yup—"

A snort and snicker escaped their mouths as they waited for her to discover the lovely white present that one of the local birds left in her perfect hair, but not a single response could be heard, that is, until she was near her car.

"I think they heard her scream in Canada," Beth laughed.

"We shouldn't be laughing," Scott struggled to catch a breath he was laughing so hard.

"I know, but it is funny," Beth inhaled. "The thing she professes to protect just pooped on her."

"I know, hard not to laugh about that."

Beth took one big intake of air and released it, along with the irritation at Valerie, the stress of running the business, and her intensifying feelings for Scott.

"How's business?" Scott asked.

"It's slow here. They have a couple of different places that people can eat. One guy criticized my choices. 'Not enough business to give us more variety?' I told him there was only so much that could be done by one person. He walked away without placing an order."

"I'm sorry, Beth. Well, I'm here. For the moment that is. I'm running the ferry today. I'll send travelers to you on the next boat. When are you leaving?"

His kindness was sweet. "It's all right, Scott. I need to remember that I will have good days and bad. Thankfully, the Coney sauce freezes well."

"Or I can come by your place and help you consume some?"

His boyish grin fought back against her idea to hold him at arm's length.

"I'll put some in a small freezer bag for you, but I'm going to be exhausted tonight, so stop by another day. It will be waiting for you. Deal?"

"Deal. I guess I will see you later then. " Crestfallen, he looked a bit pathetic as he waved goodbye and sauntered off. Beth wanted to call him back and ask him to keep her company, but she didn't trust her heart right now.

The day never improved after Scott left. No customers, no passersby, not even a person walking a dog. Beth checked the bulletin board of events that was posted in the park and found nothing happening today. *Maybe Hooper Island is quieter than the others.*

Resigned to her inevitable defeat for the day, Beth closed the window and began to pack up. She was tired, confused, and a little moody anyway. "I'd be better off at home. At least I can't cause any further damage there."

When Beth finished hooking her trailer to her Bronco, a soft breeze began to blow through the trees. Fall tried to push in, but it still felt like summer to her. The longing for the wind in her hair pushed her to take the canvas cover off the Bronco for the trip home. She had an hour drive home, and that was all the time she needed to let the wind blow away all her cares into the sea breezes.

The sun sat low in the sky, looking as ready as she felt to be tucked in for the night. A cup of lavender and honey tea would soothe her weary body, but she would need something more to calm her soul. Something that held meaning and words that brought clarity. The entire drive, she enjoyed the warmth of the sun and the glow on the horizon.

As she approached the ridge near her cottage, the glow she admired grew with intensity. A white plum highlighted the orange and red illumination that licked the sky in a menacing way while belching an acrid stench. It wasn't until she came to the top of the hill that her heart dropped to the floorboards of her Bronco.

"Oh, God. No."

14

*S*cott sat on the deck of his houseboat with a line in the water and a sweet iced tea in his hand. The day had been long, and people were brutal. Complaint after complaint flew at him as those riding the ferry had no problem telling him how awful the trip was. It didn't matter how much he tried to explain that he couldn't be responsible for the choppy waters. They still insisted on some kind of compensation.

Then there was the obvious dismissal by Beth at lunch time after Valerie all but manhandled him. He'd never felt so violated by a woman. It may have only been his second encounter with her, but he prayed it was the last.

The water slapped the sides of the boat as the breeze intensified. A hint of smoke pushed him to his feet. He scanned across the different boats docked around him as he reeled in the fishing line. He moved to the starboard, placing his pole on the table at the stern.

It wasn't until he looked up to the top of the cliff that he discovered the source of the smoke. Time slowed down as his heart froze in his chest. There, at the top of the cliff, fire engulfed a structure on Beth's property.

Scott moved into action, making his way to his truck. He made some calls as he slammed it into gear and sped from the parking lot, kicking up rocks in his wake.

"Merriweather Fire and Rescue."

"Matt, Scott here, the Merriweather cottage property has a fire."

Before Matt hung up, Scott heard the sirens go out. "We are on our way. Go make sure everyone is okay."

Without replying, Scott ended the call and tossed the phone onto the seat.

The faster Scott drove, the more impatient he became.

How could this happen?

I hope it isn't the cottage. God, don't let the fire reach the cottage.

Who would do such a thing?

An image of the mayor's menacing face flashed in his mind.

I hope he didn't.

Beth?

The last thought twisted his gut and his breathing stuttered. He couldn't imagine what he would do if Chuck Ainsley's schemes hurt her.

"Lord, she's been through enough. Keep her safe."

Scott came out of his seat a bit as he sped over the hill that stood as a barrier to the cottage. He took in the sight to assess the situation before he panicked.

The cottage was not on fire, but one of the outbuildings were. Beth's Bronco and food trailer were parked the furthest from the fire. He scanned the property for her as he got out of the truck. The night sky hung black with smoke so thick that it blurred his vision. He called for her, but there was no reply. Only the roar of the fire. The heat intensified, reaching out in all directions and wrapped its deadly fingers around him.

Movement from the side of the cottage caught his attention. Beth ran to the fire with a garden hose on at full blast. Desperation to protect her spurred him in her direction. It was in that moment he knew that he would do anything necessary to protect her.

"Beth! Beth, stay back!"

"No, it's going to get the cottage. Look!" She yelled over her shoulder and pointed to the strip of grass between the shed and the cottage. She was right; the fire licked at the stone wall of the cottage. One gust of wind and the eighteenth-century cottage would be reduced to a shell of a dwelling, weakening the mortar that held it together, destroying everything inside, and crushing Beth's heart.

"Let me. Go stand by my truck."

"No, I have it. I don't need your help. I can do this."

Her words jabbed at his heart, but only for a moment. He knew her story, her struggle to make a place for herself. She needed this place where she felt free to be who she wanted to be without the burden of her overbearing mother. This cottage, this island had become that for her. But she couldn't fight this one alone.

"Beth, let me help. You need to let me help. The fire and rescue team is on the way, but I am here now." Nothing in her posture indicated that she heard him. He put his hand on her bare shoulder and turned her to him. "Please, Beth."

Tears sprang to her eyes and she nodded, handing him the hose.

"Can you feed me some more line? It's too short."

She ran around to the side of the cottage while Scott took slow steps toward the flames. His five years as a volunteer on the fire and rescue team trained him where to direct the water effectively.

He sprayed the roof of the cottage to keep the flames off, as well as the grass that began to smolder. The barn was already a loss, so keeping the dwelling safe was his number one priority until he heard the sounds of the cavalry approaching. He glanced over his shoulder in time to see them crest the hill and make the final descent toward the fire. Other volunteer trucks and cars followed soon after.

Beth came up beside him with a wet shirt that had hung around her waist when he arrived. She tied it around his nose and mouth to offer protection from smoke inhalation. He sent her a look of thanks and her teary eyes replied, saying a bit more than thank you. He watched as one of the volunteers swept her away while others moved in with a much bigger and more powerful hose.

"We have it from here, Scott. Let a medic look at you," the commander shouted.

Scott did as ordered, with more reluctance than a willingness to obey, but the tightness forming in his chest warned him to be wise.

Once at the emergency vehicle, he found Beth sitting on the back bumper with a breathing mask and soot on her face and tears in her eyes. He sat next to her, his arm touching hers but not embracing her.

"Mr. Anderson, can we take your vitals?" one of the EMT's asked. He knew the protocol, so he removed his flannel over-shirt. At that movement, Beth's eyes turned on him and widened at the sight. He held back a smirk, but he could see her observation of him in only jeans and a white tank. She turned her head away the moment their eyes met.

He watched his teammates put out the flames as an EMT took his blood pressure, listened to his heart and lungs, and hooked him up with a breathing mask as well. Apparently, he inhaled more smoke than he thought.

"I don't know how it happened," Beth muttered though the mask. "I don't store anything in there that could spontaneously combust. The shed was clean."

"No paint supplies or anything?" Scott asked, hoping that his hunch was wrong, and it was an accident.

"I haven't had time to do any work to it, not that I didn't

88

want to. When I moved in, the shed was completely empty. I thought about making it a little bigger to house the trailer actually. In case there was an off season."

At that moment, Mayor Ainsley had the nerve to approach Beth. He placed his hand on her shoulder, sympathy in his eyes. "I am so sorry this happened. Maybe next time you should take better care of things."

Without further explanation or apology, he turned and walked away, a smug expression on his face.

Shock registered on the faces of everyone who heard his words. The man had nerve.

Scott stood and took off the mask and flung it into the ambulance, then marched right to the pudgy bully. "Chuck!" Scott shouted. "How'd you do it?"

The mayor turned to Scott, an evil grin spreading across his face. "I have no idea what you could be referring to?"

"The fire, how did you do it? You are too self-centered to do it yourself, so who did it for you?"

"I still cannot believe that you think I am this devious."

Scott took another step closer so that no one else heard what was said. "I'll tell these good people your plan for this house and the target you have had on that innocent woman this whole time. You'll not get away with this."

Charles pointed his stubby finger right in the middle of Scott's chest and poked him. "You will say no such thing, because all I have to do is tell them you are a disgruntled employee trying to blackmail me. Then I'll tell that little lady friend of yours that you knew about this all along. And then you, my dear boy, will be gone. I told you a long time ago I needed dedication from my employees, and you did not give me that."

"The people won't believe you."

"Maybe, but it will plant doubt in that Yankee freeloader's mind, and she'll never see you as anything other than algae on the reef. So, if you're smart, which I highly doubt, you'll keep your mouth shut."

Without giving Scott a chance to refute, the mayor turned and walked away.

Stunned and a little beaten down, Scott turned to head back to Beth while working hard not to meet her gaze. He knew the man could ruin him. He was conniving and manipulative. Power hungry, even. Sure, Scott had nothing to do with the fire, but Charles Ainsley would tell any lie necessary to make him come out smelling like a peach pie. Even pin a fire on an innocent man. He had witnessed the man do much worse to get what he wanted.

Scott felt her eyes on him, yet he refused to look at her. He was pinned between what was right and his reputation. He had to choose which was more important. If he chose to not provoke the mayor, then a future with Beth could remain a possibility. If he told her what he knew about the man's plans, that she had a target on her, then he could lose her for good.

His steps faltered as he approached her, her perfectly painted pink toes coming into his downcast view. She took hold of his hand, and the pain of what he knew was right stabbed him.

He gazed at her face, searing every feature into his memory. Finally, the affectionate look in her eyes was the one he had longed to see, and he was never going to see it again. All because he kept this one detail from her.

Scott took a deep breath and let the words fly. "Mayor Ainsley set the fire."

Her tender gaze disappeared with one sentence.

"How do you know?"

"He asked me two weeks ago to help him push you out. He wants the cottage so he can turn it into a historical marker, a museum maybe, so that he can make money off of it, I suppose. Obviously, I told him no, but I didn't think he would go this far."

Distrust and anger flashed in her green eyes. She rose to her feet. "I can't handle this right now, Scott. I wish you would have told me earlier."

He watched her walk over to the fire marshal, her arms crossed over her upper body like a shield. He'd let her down by not informing her of the potential danger and the guilt of that slammed into him. Somehow, he would make this right.

Journal Entry
  October 25ᵗʰ
  That was close. Almost too close. But it was Scott's confession after the fire that has my head spinning. I know that he would never be part of something like this, but he knew someone wanted me to leave. He then kept that information from me. I don't know if I should be mad or cut him some slack.

  I do know that I was pretty crazy during the fire. I have never jumped in front of danger like that before. I play it safe. I color within the lines. Maybe it is all part of this "independence" journey Gram asked me to embark on.

  Man, I wish Gram was here. She would tell me what to do.
  Beth

15

*S*leep would not come to her so when the sun peeked its head up over the blanket of water, Beth poured herself one more cup of coffee, tightened her navy-blue robe around her waist, and walked outside. The air still held hints of the previous night's fire, but the fresh sea air helped to wash away the worst hints of burning plastic.

What remained of the shed was the metal roof sitting on top of ash and soot. For once, she was glad she sold everything she owned back in Michigan. She couldn't lose what she didn't have.

Just like Scott.

Scott's confession rang in her ears now like it did through the night. *"He wanted me to help him push you out,"* he said. No matter how hard her heart and mind battled, one side, the side of reason, always won. Scott was asked, but he hadn't agreed. There had to be more to the story.

Beth picked up her phone, scrolled through her contacts in search of his name. Just as she was about to tap the call icon, the device vibrated in her hand and her dad's face appeared.

Talking to him could be the best thing for her at the

moment; he was a voice of reason during many disputes between her and her mother. Maybe she could get some guy input on the situation.

She tapped the answer icon.

"Hi, Dad?"

"Hey, Pumpkin. How are you doing down there?"

If she told him about the fire, he would insist she come home.

"Everything is going well."

"Is it proving to be everything you hoped it would?"

She wasn't sure how to answer that one. It felt a little more like a loaded question.

"Things are definitely not what I was expecting, but nothing I regret right now."

"Well, that's good. I miss you. Things are much different up here now that Gram is gone. She was the glue, I think."

A tear sprang to life.

"I miss her, too. There are times, when I am prepping food for the next day, I think I hear her telling me how much of this and how little of that I need to put in the recipe. When I turn to see if she is there, I only find an empty room."

"People we love have a way of imprinting on our hearts and our lives. Your mom really is lost without her parents here. It's sad to watch, really."

Beth wanted to ask him why he didn't step up to the plate, be the husband, the head of the family, and talk to her mother. She wouldn't though, because she wasn't sure she could be respectful about it. The wound her mother left on Beth was too raw.

"I know I should say something to her. I just don't know where to begin."

Well, at least he knew better.

"I understand, Dad. She isn't easy. Anyway, how is everyone else?"

After a few minutes of small talk, he finally divulged his reason for calling.

"So, before I go, when are you going to tell me about the fire?"

"It's no big deal, Dad. It was only a shed fire, and it's all taken care of now. I'm calling the insurance agent today. I got this."

She wouldn't tell him, but if there was some way that he could come and make this all better she would welcome it at this point. Beth had to do this on her own though. She'd be thirty in a couple years. It was time to step up and be an adult.

"Okay. Well, I love you, Pumpkin. Be safe."

"I will, Dad. I love you. Tell everyone I said hello."

"I will." And the line went quiet.

She would take care of herself, too. There was no reason, besides her father, to ever go home again. She had a business, money, a home, and food. What more could she need?

Love, family...

The two things that make life worth living. She had to admit that coming home to an empty cottage was getting to be a little dreary. There was nothing to look forward to at the end of the workday.

"Maybe I should get a dog."

Except it couldn't be around the food and wouldn't be able to go with her as she traveled the islands. She made a mental note to talk to the council about it at the next meeting. If they gave the green light, then a phone call to Kendall, who was a veterinarian, she would be able to answer Beth's questions about finding the right dog.

A knock on the front door startled Beth from her thoughts.

"Why would someone be knocking on my door this early?" Beth looked down at herself and smoothed out her hair. "I haven't even cleaned up yet."

Beth went to the door, hoping that Scott wasn't on the other side. He would be in for a fright if he was, and she wasn't sure she could ever face him again. Thankfully, Mallory graced her front steps with two lidded disposable cups and a box of something that smelled sweet and delicious. Her friend looked like she had just stepped out of the pages of some nautical magazine.

"Well, hello there." Beth gestured to herself. "I haven't even showered yet, so forgive my bed head and bathrobe. And because you come bearing the best thing in the world right now, you have solidified yourself into the best friend category."

They giggled at the exaggeration despite holding more truth than Mallory would ever know. The kindness nearly overwhelmed her.

"Think nothing of it." Mallory entered the living room, "I just wanted to check on you. I heard you had an exciting evening. It looks like a war zone out there."

"I thought you spent Wednesdays on Hopper. What are you doing here?"

"I have time to get there. I have to drive past here anyway. Besides, you're more important right now. Things have been slow enough lately that they won't even be waiting for me."

"Thank you," replied Beth as she fought against the lump forming in her throat and the water pooling in her eyes, "for caring so much."

Mallory put an arm around Beth and guided her to the couch. "You are most welcome, darlin'." *She sounds a bit like Uncle Bud. Will she call me sugar next?* "But it looks like you need to download. Now, where do you keep your plates for these muffins?"

Beth rose to help her friend, but Mallory stopped. "I'll get it. You just rest."

"All right." Beth pointed to the proper cupboard as she relented control of the kitchen.

While Mallory busied around the room, Beth pulled herself together. She didn't want to completely lose all control on her friend.

"So, what happened?"

Beth told her the previous days' troubles, about coming home to the shed in flames, about Scott's heroic attempt to help until fire and rescue arrived. No matter how much she didn't want to discuss the confrontation Scott had with the mayor and his confession, the words flowed like they had a mind of their own. By the time she finished unloading, Beth held a shredded Kleenex and her face was soaked.

"Mallory, I just don't think I can do this. It's like I'm going through the motions. And don't even get me started on how I feel about Scott."

"Let's talk about Scott for a minute. His confession might explain why I saw him where I did this morning."

"Where was that?"

"On the ferry headed for Mimosa. I asked him where he was headed in passing. He said he had business in Georgia."

"I wonder what business he has there. Anyway, it isn't important." Beth brushed it off, but her curiosity kept the bit of information in the forefront of her mind.

"So, Scott. What's going on there?" Mallory persisted.

"He's my friend. A friend who kept something from me, and the cottage almost burned down because of it."

"Don't you think Scott might have a reason? And if you think he is just a friend, you're going to have to be more convincing. The way you two look at each other displays something more than just friendship."

"It's all it can be, so let's leave it alone."

Mallory gave her a scolding look. "You don't have to tell me, but you do need to examine your own heart on it—be honest with yourself."

"Now, tell me why you think you can't keep going on with *Comfort Cuisine*. It's a hit throughout the islands. I hear about it all over the place, even on Mimosa. You have a real talent for crafting great meals that are easy to handle on the go."

Beth leaned back in the couch, resigning to the need to have the conversation she had been avoiding.

"I'm not sure how much rejection I can take. I have lived most of my life being told I'm not good enough by my mother and sisters. I can't handle strangers telling me the same."

Mallory turned in her seat to give Beth more of her attention. Face to face, Beth saw the compassion in her friend's eyes. Compassion that she missed.

"You're making me wonder if you even prayed about this."

Beth could only remain silent as the statement hit her, hard.

"Um, Beth, if coming down here was just a way to escape family or to try to make your Gram happy, then you might as well just move on back."

Beth swallowed hard to force the coffee and muffin in her stomach to stay down.

"But the Beth I know is passionate about food. She turns food into art because of a love that wells up inside. God gave you that. Use it for His glory wherever He sends you—I just hope it really was here. Now, if this is truly a passion, make these beautiful creations so that you can share the love with others. Stay, fight, and let people help you. God places a talent and a passion in each of us, so we are to use it for His glory. Don't turn your back on that."

Beth rolled her words around for a moment. Was this move something she was supposed to have done or just a misguided whim?

"You're right, Mallory. I told Gram years ago that this was something I wanted to do, but I was too afraid to do it. She told me I needed to use this gift for Him and I haven't. I've just been going through the motions."

"Grief does weird things to us, Beth. Trust me. I get that. It takes time to get through that. But if this has been a problem since before your gram died, then it's time to do a whole lot more prayin'."

"That is something I haven't done since her death. Even after Scott and I talked about this very thing right after I arrived. I put God on the back burner. I have been doing things my way in search of independence from my family, and not once have I pulled out the Bible Gram gave me to read or spent time praying for God's direction."

Beth leaned over and wrapped Mallory in a hug. "Thank you so much. I know what I'll be doing today."

"Good." Mallory disengaged herself from Beth's clutches and gave her a teasing look. "And pray about Scott. Talk to him. You might be surprised."

Journal Entry
   October 26th
   Thank you, God, for sending Mallory.
   I have been blind. Forgive me, please.
   Beth

$\mathcal{S}$cott hated the ridiculously long process to unload the ferry. He hated the drive to Savannah. He hated coming to the mainland, period. If Scott couldn't find what he needed on one of the islands, then he didn't need it. Today's visit to Savannah was necessary, and there was nothing that would stop him from doing what was right.

He'd lain awake half the night praying for wisdom on what to do. The answer came right away, but instead of giving in to God's gentle push, Scott battled with it. It might just be hearsay, and he had no proof of anything, but his buddies with the Savannah police might be able to do a little digging for him—at least enough to make it worth the trip. If he made the wrong move, more innocent people would get hurt.

Scott pulled his truck into the furthest parking spot from the door to the building. Before he even reached to turn off the truck, he bent his head in prayer. This investigation needed to go well.

When he exited the truck, his pulled out his phone as he walked through the parking lot, hoping for some notification from Beth. He understood her being upset with him; he'd kept important information from her. The lingering silence from her, or how much it bothered him, was unexpected.

"It's about time you got here," a male voice boomed from the steps leading to the station. "You must drive like an old lady," Blake Andrews clapped him on the back and shook Scott's hand when he approached.

"The ferry was extra slow today. Not sure what the holdup was." He would omit the part about driving five under the speed limit the whole way there.

"Naw, you drove five under, didn't you? You hate coming over here." Jacob Andrews gave him a pointed glare.

"Okay, 'you two.' Knock it off. Can we get this over with? Then we can catch up?"

Scott watched the identical twin brothers glance at one another and shrug. "Okay, Mr. Anderson, let's talk." Blake turned and led the way, and Jacob followed with Scott close behind.

They took him to one of the interrogation rooms with cinder block walls, a table, three chairs, and a two-way mirror. The fluorescent light overhead buzzed at a decibel worthy of nails down a chalkboard.

"So, are you two gonna play 'good cop, bad cop' or just talk?" Scott asked, half joking.

"Depends. Do you have some confessing to do?" Jacob replied.

Scott took a minute to draw out his answer as he sat on the one side, rubbed the stress out of his face, and placed his hands on the table. "Sort of."

"Well, is it something you should have a lawyer here for? You know, just in case." Blake's steely look would make a hardened criminal confess.

"No, it's not that bad. At least not on my part. Listen, can I just tell you and let you two decide?"

The brothers nodded in unison as Jacob pushed a button on

a recorder and Blake took the cap off his pen so he could take notes on a yellow notepad. They drew out every move, and he knew it was just to get under his skin.

Scott, a forever resident of the islands, and the Andrews boys, Savannah natives, met at church camp on Skye Island around the time he'd also met Beth. They were only together for the summers but when they came together for camp, it was like no time had passed. Even into adulthood, they kept in touch.

"You may begin," Blake mocked. His face still straight, but his eyes teased.

For the next hour, Scott revealed all the details of his conversations with Charles Ainsley, the things the man asked of him, schemes he hatched, and his confession to Scott last night.

"So, he flat out told you that he set the fire?" Jacob asked.

"No, he said that because I refused him, he found someone to do it for him."

"Did you know he was going to set fire to her property before?'

"No. He wanted to discuss a plan, but I refused to help him cause any more damage."

"Did you tell the property owner?" Blake asked this time.

"Yes. She saw the heated exchange and asked. I'm not about to lie to her."

"But you withheld information from her that the mayor did not like how she came to claim the coveted property?"

"Trust me, I am still beating myself up over that one."

The brothers gave each other a glance. They would grill him about that later.

Jacob reached over and stopped the recording, and Blake put the pen down.

"We'll do some snooping, but we can't make promises. There is no evidence, Scott. Just your word against his." Jacob gave him an apologetic look. "Next time you coax a confession, record it."

Blake dropped the cool cop act. "Now can we go eat?"

Scott rose. "I'm game, and starving actually."

They pulled into the strip mall parking lot and Scott's mouth began to water. Wiley's Championship BBQ had some of the best ribs, brisket, and chicken he'd ever tasted. Maybe even better than Beth's, but he wouldn't tell her that. Then again, he'd eat anything smoked or grilled to "fall off the bone" perfection and slathered in barbecue sauce.

The moment they'd seated themselves and placed their orders, a different kind of interrogation started.

"So, this Elizabeth Stevens, is she the same one you had a summer thing with in high school?" Blake asked between sips of his Cherry Coke.

"Yeah, why?"

"I was just wondering."

"You got this little twinkle in your eye every time you brought her up. Does she know you still have a thing for her?" Jacob's question left Scott wondering himself.

"I don't know, but she has made it clear that I am in the friend zone."

The brothers groaned. "That is the worst place to be when you love someone that much," Blake said.

"I don't even know the extent of my own feelings. How can you claim to know the exact measure?"

"We're detectives, Scott. We see things." Jacob gave Scott a smug look.

"Well, I can't think about that right now. She's hurting and has made her stance very clear."

"For now," Blake waggled his eyebrows. "You can change her mind, you know? There is nothing wrong in prayerfully pursuing her. I think it says something that after all these years, you still have a thing for her."

"Or it is nostalgia?" Scott asked.

Ready to be finished with this discussion, Scott changed the topics to their wives, Tina and Liz, and their growing families. He hoped that if he got them talking about themselves for a bit, they would leave him alone when it came to Beth.

Three hours later, they said their goodbyes back at the station. Scott invited the guys to bring their families out for a little vacation...or investigation, and he would show them around.

Back on the ferry to Mimosa, instead of watching the ocean horizon as he typically did, he stayed in his truck, thinking about his first encounter with Beth a few months ago. The smile on her face as the ocean spray dampened her skin felt like a punch in the gut, but in all the right ways. Now, he wondered if that was an act, or a fleeting moment of peace, on her part.

He wanted to help her, to be there for her, but she was just as stubborn as she was a troublemaker. And boy, did he love her kind of trouble because it almost always involved him. There wasn't anything he wouldn't do to show her how much he wanted her in his life. If only she wasn't so afraid to let him in.

Scott pondered on the things she revealed to him, and the reasons for her fear became clearer. She was told how out of place and unwanted she was by people who were supposed to love her unconditionally. They put labels and restrictions on her, forcing her into a box. A box of inadequacy and fake personalities, until she went to visit her Gram. Now Gram was gone, and Beth was left floating in a sea of uncertainty.

He rested his arm on the windowsill of the truck and leaned his head into his hand. Pressure began to build behind his eyes and his sinuses closed. His heart sat like a rock in his chest, the weight of the revelation beating it into his ribs. When at last he couldn't contain the hurt for her, the prick of tears let loose.

"God, it's just not right. She is such a beautiful person. She doesn't deserve this. What can I do to help her see? Is there even anything I can do? I'm not You. I can't heal or restore what has been taken from her, but I'm willing to help."

Then it dawned on him. He could be the conduit in which God moved so that she understood her value and how loved she truly was.

A plan took form as the tears dried. To carry it out would take great patience, but he wanted her whole, not for his sake but for hers. It would mean he had to slow things down. God would have to flood him with some self-control. Her sense of value in God's eyes was more important than him wanting her in his life forever.

Beth was worth the wait.

17

*V*alerie approached the door of the mayor's office after a week of icing her sprained ankle. If she had known how dangerous setting a shed on fire would be, she would have refused the mayor's plan, but fear and desperation will make a person do dangerous things.

The mayor called her three times a day. Each call she ignored. Fear of the man was outgrowing her fear of not having what she desired most. She never realized what the man was capable of. He always seemed so harmless. But here she was, trembling in front of his door waiting for the fire to consume her for the rotten thing she'd done.

"Enter!" the man bellowed.

Valerie took a deep breath to calm her nerves and put on her confident face, hoping he didn't see through her act. When she opened the door, she found the mayor poised behind his desk in his high back leather chair, a lowball glass holding ice and an amber liquid propped in his hand. A cigar hung precariously out the side of his mouth. An imposing man dressed in a sharp business suit sat with his back to the door and looked to be doing the same as the mayor.

The room reeked of tobacco and liquor, forcing images of her past to the forefront of her mind. All she wanted to do was run. Men and alcohol were not a good mix in her experience but running was not an option this time. She would be strong and firm in her approach. The last thing she wanted was to show him how afraid he made her.

"Well, it's about time. Where have you been?"

"Forgive me, Mr. Ainsley, sir. I hurt myself," her gaze shifted between the two men. Unsure what the other man knew, she did her best to cover up her activities. "I stepped wrong and sprained my ankle last week. It took longer to heal than usual."

"If you would wear shoes like a normal woman, maybe you wouldn't have hurt yourself. You live on an island, for Pete's sake. Wear some sandals."

She could feel the pressure of tears building behind her eyes at the condescending tone. Only one other man talked to her that way, and the day he died in a house fire was the day she found her independence from the abuse. *So why would you sign on with another man just like him?*

"I guess I like them. What can I do for you, Mr. Ainsley?"

"I want to introduce you to your partner. His name is Mr. Black. You two will be working together on the next phase of this evacuation plan."

The man in the suit, Mr. Black, stood and put his hand out to her. His firm jaw clenched at the sight of her, and his eyes flashed with a sinister gleam, but his smile softened all his menacing features. "It's a pleasure to meet you, Miss ..."

"Just call me Valerie."

"All right then, Valerie. I look forward to working with you." He glanced down her figure and back up to her eyes. The action gave her the sensation of an army of tiny spiders traveling from his hand to hers, up her arm and down the rest of her body. "Yes, I think we will work nicely together, Chuck," he said over his shoulder without taking his eyes off her. "I'll do the heavy lifting from now on, Valerie. You just play the distraction."

She could easily agree to that.

"Oh, she will be a happy distraction for sure. Now, have a seat. I want to share my plan with you."

Valerie took a seat, but a question nagged in the back of her mind. "Before you get started, can I just ask why you just don't kick her off the property?"

"Oh, you simple-minded woman." She would ignore the jab, for now. "I cannot just kick her off her land. It is legally hers. It was signed over to her by her grandmother, who is a descendent of this island's founder. She needs to be persuaded that she is not wanted or needed here—that it would be better for her to go back to Michigan."

"I know all this. It doesn't answer my question, though. Why is it so important to you? There is nothing exciting about her land. I don't know anyone who would pay to see it or stay at the cottage." She watched the man squirm in his chair, telling her she was onto something. "There is more you're not saying, isn't there?"

The two men shifted their eyes to each other. A knowing look passed between them. She suddenly second-guessed how involved she really wanted to be.

"What do you think, Mr. Black? Should we let her in on the plan?"

The quiet man pierced Valerie with his steely glare with his large arms crossed over his chest. "She could be useful."

His words paired with his demeanor chilled the blood in her veins.

"I agree. I think she only needs to know her part but not what we are after," he spoke to Mr. Black like she wasn't even there. "Agree?"

The man only replied with a nod.

"Well, Ms. Hornigold? You in?"

Was sharing her life with Scott and getting rid of Elizabeth worth her life? At this stage of the game, Scott hardly acknowledged her presence. If this went well, would he even still see her while she struggled with a guilty conscience? She looked out the window to her right with the open sea not far away. If only the answer was written in the sky to give her some direction.

"Time is ticking, and I have places to be. What is your answer?"

A squeak of a voice in the back of her mind warned her not to agree, but her curiosity won.

She straightened in her chair and gave each man a pointed look. "I've already begun the dirty work, so I'm in."

Both men flashed her an ominous grin as Mayor Ainsley explained her part in the plan.

"You're a woman who knows how to, shall we say, get attention."

"So, you want me to be a decoy?"

The mayor nodded. "But not just that, you will be getting your hands dirty. You're obviously smaller than Mr. Black and he'll need your assistance."

"And what are we looking for?"

Again, the men glanced at each other. Mr. Black shook his head.

"You'll know when it's found."

She wanted to push for more information, but the look in his eyes told her not to push.

"So, what do we get out of this?" Mr. Black asked. She wondered the same.

"I'll give each of you ten percent. No more, no less," Mayor Ainsley declared as he leaned back in the chair, looking as if he had won a boxing match.

Mr. Black shot her a look; one she took as an encouragement to get in the negotiations. One minute he tried to intimidate her, another he encouraged her?

"I say twenty a piece, or we walk and find it our own way," she said, waiting for him to turn her down.

Mayor Ainsley looked between her and Mr. Black, stood to his feet with a glare in his eyes. He held his hand out to her first. She rose and took hold of it. *That was too easy.* She'd expected a fight back or something. *Watch yourself.*

"You have a deal, my dear." He then turned to Mr. Black. "Now, I will see you both in one week, and we'll begin."

Valerie and Mr. Black made their way outside. Once in the sun, she thought for sure that its rays would warm her, but all she felt was a chill that permeated to her bones. Her soul felt even more empty than the moment she walked in. What did it matter, though? She was caught in the scheme before she ever knew the plan. There was no use fighting it now.

"I'll tell you what," Mr. Black's breath grazed her neck as he stepped closer. "How about we go back to my room at the inn up the street and discuss adjustments to the mayor's plan. There's no reason we can't find a way to turn this into a two-way, split-profit proposition? As a Hornigold, the land and everything on it, should really belong to you."

He was talking her lingo now, and his dark eyes and bad boy appeal were something that could work to her advantage—more so than the slimy, smelly mayor. She would not go to his room though. Bad things happened in strange men's rooms. She had enough street smarts to deflect his plan.

"How about a walk down by the docks? It is late enough that there won't be anyone around, but not so private that you would be compelled to do things I might not appreciate," she teased and purred enough to get him to follow her lead without getting herself into trouble.

"You are a persuasive one." He took hold of her hand and

placed it in the crook of his elbow. "Explains how the mayor just caved to you."

Yes, she did know how to be persuasive, but did she like the woman she was becoming?

18

*A*nytime Beth missed the flavors of home, she made a point to include them on the weekly menu. Some weeks, such as when it was the end of baseball season, hot dogs in all forms made the shortlist as thoughts of the Detroit Tigers playing at Comerica Park played in her head. Now that the football season was in play, sub sandwiches and, Michigan favorite, pasties were at the top of her list. Since anyone could get a sub sandwich down here, she picked pasties for the week.

In frilly letters, Beth wrote out the specials of the week on the folding chalkboard, smiling at the list. Delicious, Upper Peninsula inspired, hand-held pies stuffed with ground beef and pork, red potatoes, rutabagas, and all the savory seasonings were a perfect on-the-go meal for Comfort Cuisine. Pairing it with a Coke made for a great weekly special. Now she had to figure out which Coke to serve.

A flash of a young, ruddy faced Scott as he consumed his first pasty came to mind. An ache over not hearing from him this last week and a half dulled her excitement to make the meat pies. Beth could hardly keep herself from calling him or taking a ferry ride just to talk to him. She longed for the gentle companionship he offered, but the fire confession seemed to have ruined it.

Not only were her emotions a mess, her clientele kept shrinking. If she'd been in Michigan, she would understand because the weather would be cold and wet right now. The temperatures on the islands had only felt marginally cooler since she arrived in August, although evidence of Christmas was beginning to show up on many homes. With Thanksgiving being only a week away, that had to be the explanation for the decline.

Just as soon as she resolved to stay on Merriweather Island, she received a phone call from her eldest sister. "As the eldest daughter," Barbara declared, "I feel like it is my duty to persuade you to forget this silly idea and come home. You have been at this for almost three full months now and Daddy said you are having issues there. Your safety is clearly in danger. Just come home, even if it is for the holidays." Beth stood her ground with her decision, much to the irritation of her sister.

When she went out to the Bronco to make her way to Elnora Island for the day, a flat tire on the trailer greeted her. She was prepared, though. Just last weekend, the new tires that she ordered for the trailer and her Bronco had arrived. That same day, Andrew Mikels, a local builder, stopped by and offered to build her a new storage building. And he built it further from the cottage. It was a lot to take in, but she was grateful for his kindness and her preparedness.

Yet, here she sat, ready to serve the residents of Elnora and no one was around. She stood from creating her menu sign for the day and surveyed the area around her. There had to be people around here that wanted something other than diner food for their lunch break.

From a distance, she heard the roar of the approaching ferry, along with the shouts of workers on the pier as they made ready for the boat to dock. She searched for a familiar face, one in particular, but was saddened to see only a handful of people step off.

A small group of women passed, making their way to the park with their children. She greeted them in a welcoming manner, but instead of a returned "Hello," they glared in her direction and proceeded to whisper to one another. "What are we, in junior high?" she muttered.

Sometime later, another water taxi made its way toward the slip. This one carrying bicycles, and more people than the last.

Determination burned within her, and Beth greeted passengers as they passed by. Not to sell, but to just be friendly. That's when she heard it.

"Isn't that the woman who took another woman's man?"

"Homewrecker."

"Yeah, I think that's the one. She's from somewhere up north."

"Why would she even come down here? Can't she sell her junk up there?"

"I heard she was kicked out by her family."

"Didn't she cause a fire on Merriweather?"

"I'm not sure she caused it, but I did hear that she has had private meetings with Merriweather's mayor. If you know what I mean."

The entire time she heard each statement, her stomach swirled a little more, but the last lie made her want to lose everything in her stomach.

"Well, what on earth are you doing here?" Valerie screeched from the sidewalk.

Beth took a deep breath, calming the growing irritation. "Last I checked, it is a free country, Valerie. I am allowed to be here."

Valerie shifted back and forth, glancing to the front and around the other side of the trailer.

"Are you looking for something? Is there something you would like to eat?"

"No, I'm good. I'm just here to meet a friend."

She continued to pace back and forth in front of Beth, her composure faltering with each pass. Something was up, but what?

At last, Valerie's eyes brightened on something just out of Beth's view. Her eyes shifted back to Beth as a smile bloomed on the woman's face. Then the object of Valerie's attention came into view, and what a sight he was. Tall, tan, chiseled, and the size of a house. He sported all black attire and a million-dollar smile.

"Hello, darling. I hope I didn't keep you too long." He embraced Valerie and placed an unexpectedly chaste kiss on her cheek.

"Think nothing of it, sweetie. Let's get out of here," Valerie glanced at her through slit eyes. "We don't want to hang around this dumpy trailer longer than necessary."

"I guess she got over Scott," she mumbled.

As if her thoughts summoned him from nowhere, Scott plopped himself right in front of her window.

The excitement of seeing a friendly face bubbled inside.

"Well, hello stranger."

Scott looked at the menu and that grin she loved so much spread across his face. "You made pasties this week? Woman, I'm going to have to make you buy me new clothes. My belt is getting tight."

Without thinking, she scanned down and back up to his face. "You look fine to me."

Crimson patches formed around his neck and up to his ears, and Beth couldn't help but smile. *Dial it back girl. Remember, you don't want a man, you want a friend.*

Scott cleared his throat, shifted his stance, and chuckled. "Anyway, what do I have to do to get a couple of those?"

"Give me five dollars."

"The sign says five each, so I only get one?" Scott pushed out his bottom lip in a pout and something thumped inside of her. If he left that lip out there much longer, she might start thinking things she shouldn't want to.

"No, I'll give you two. I'm about to close up. Plus, I know you love them." Beth turned her back to him, hoping he didn't see the flash of self-doubt she suddenly felt at the statement *I'm about to close up.*

"Seems a bit early for you. Is everything okay?"

She struggled with whether or not to tell him about the day, or even the week, while she warmed his pasties. The last thing Scott needed was for her to blow her lid in front of him.

"Oh, no worries. Today has just been an interesting day. All I would like to do right now is go home, curl up in my fluffy blanket with a long book, and just forget this past week. Maybe even the past nine months." The last part was more for herself than for Scott to hear.

A strong masculine hand touched her forearm, offering peace instead of startling her. She hadn't heard him open the door to her trailer, but it didn't matter. "You're rambling, Beth. I don't think you're okay." His usual playfulness was replaced with a subtle affection that wrapped around her like a hug. Nothing flirty or hinting at anything other than friendship came from his lips.

"You're right. I'm not all right."

"Do you want to talk?"

His offer touched her heart, but she also knew that going home and hiding out for a little while was all she needed right now.

She continued to package his order, adding a couple of extra goodies, just to thank him for his kindness.

"No," she turned to him, offering him the to-go box, using it as a barrier between them. "I thank you for being concerned.

You have no idea how much I value our friendship. I never want that to change."

He took the box, his fingers skimming across hers, sending shivers up her arm and down her back straight to her toes. "Promise me that you will call me if you need to talk." She didn't answer right away. "I mean it, Beth. Please call me if you need anything."

"I promise. Thank you."

Scott kept his hand over hers as they both held on to the box of meat pies. His green eyes pinned her in place with all the tenderness she knew he was capable of displaying. For the first time in months, she saw love looking back at her and a small part of her wanted to fall into the arms that he would open wide for her.

"I need to close up, and I'm sure you have a ferry to get on. I'll call you soon." She put on her best face and squeezed past Scott, pulling him toward the door.

"Okay, okay, I get your hint. Are you always this stubborn?"

"Only with you, Scotty." She couldn't help but chuckle. "Only when I'm with you."

An hour later, Beth backed the Bronco up to the hitch of the trailer, jumped out, turned the crank to lower the trailer on the ball hitch, then went to the back of the trailer to raise the support legs. It was tedious work and made her work up a sweat in the cooling fall breeze, but it kept her mind and body busy. The rapid activity kept away thoughts about Scott or the fire or Valerie.

Once she hit the road to Merriweather, she let the music from the latest album of her favorite worship team fill all the cracks of her heart as cars passed by. All the songs resonated in her spirit, healing those raw areas inside. From one island to the next, her mind only focused on the words to each song. Before she knew it, she'd almost reached the hill at the edge of her property.

The Bronco sped up quicker than usual as she came down the hill. Beth pressed the brakes, but nothing happened. She pressed the brake pedal again, and still nothing happened. Looking out the windshield she tried to gage where she could go and how far she had left before she went over the edge of the cliff. With only a couple of yards left, her options were limited.

"Oh, Jesus."

Just as the edge of the cliff left her view, she made a sharp turn to the right and went around behind the cottage while praying that she didn't tip or jackknife the trailer. Beth bounced in her seat as the Bronco and trailer took several bumps and she took one more hard right. She passed the front of the house as the Bronco began to slow. She pressed the brake pedal a few more times, praying all the while for another miracle.

Just as she turned the wheel to the right a third time to drive by the back of the cottage again, everything stopped. The engine turned off and the keys fell against her foot on the floorboard. She wasn't sure if she turned the Bronco off or if Someone came to her aid. It didn't matter, though. She was alive and nothing else was damaged, except the brakes.

"Thank you, Lord."

But all the thanks in the world didn't change that she needed time. Time to pray, time to think, time to decide what to do next.

Leaving the Bronco and trailer right where they sat, she put the cover back on the vehicle, locked everything up, and made her way to the cottage. She didn't want to deal with whatever had gone wrong right now. She just needed time.

Journal Entry
November 19th
Something happened today, and I really needed to talk to you, but I

couldn't call you. I couldn't sit at your kitchen island with a cup of tea and share how afraid I am or how confused Scott makes me. I wish you were here, even for a moment, because I really need to hear your voice. You knew all the right things to say, and now I am alone in this world and I don't know what to do.

Father, send help, please.

Beth

19

*N*o one should be alone on the holidays. Every home should be full of food and laughter. At least that is what his mama always told him. Yet, here it was, his second Thanksgiving without either of his parents, and he was precisely that—alone. Scott typically attempted to have friends over, but this year the weight of what and who were missing hung heavy around his neck.

He baked his own turkey breast, made a small green bean casserole, dumped out canned cranberry jelly, and fluffed some instant stuffing. All that was missing was the pie Gram always sent down to him. Her cranberry apple pie with basket woven crust. It was the one thing he always looked forward to. It would not come this year.

He sat at the dinner table, ready to gorge himself on his feast for one, and bowed his head to give thanks.

"Heavenly Father, I give You thanks for all the blessings you have bestowed on me this year. I pray that I will continue to walk in Your ways as I interact with those around me. Now bless this food to my body and give me clarity to understand this mood I am in. In Jesus' name. Amen."

With knife in one hand and fork in the other, Scott made his first cut into the turkey. That's when, around mid-chew of the first satisfying bite, a thought hit him square in the chest.

If you are feeling it, one of your brothers or sisters could be as well.

It was something his father told him many times when he expressed that he was feeling a certain emotion. The phrase held truth in many ways, so Scott recalled every person in his life who could be having a hard time today. Each person he mentally checked off because he knew they had some place to be or were with someone.

Then there was her. He pictured her delicate features, petite frame, hair the color of chocolate that hung to her waist, and those golden eyes. Beth was always the first person he thought of, until a week ago.

She made sure he knew she didn't need or want his help, and his heart had grown too fond of having her near all the time. Scott gave her the space she asked for but now that he was thinking about her, he couldn't recall seeing *Comfort Cuisines* on any of the islands since that day on Elnora.

Leaving the hot meal, he went to his room to fetch his cell phone off the side table. His thumbs moved over the keypad as he sent her a text message. He only waited thirty seconds for a reply before he dialed her number.

As the phone rang, he paced. It rang again, and he grumbled. It went to voicemail, and concern began to take over. Knowing the extremes the mayor was willing to go in order to get her to leave, Scott resolved to make a house call.

He packed up the feast, grabbed keys, and ran to the truck. He was not about to let her spend today alone.

During the twenty-minute drive to Beth's cottage, Scott called her phone more times than he could count. Not once did she answer as each time the call sent him to voicemail.

He wasn't sure what he would find when he arrived but seeing the trailer behind the cottage was not it. Beth always parked off to one side. He even tried to get her to lay pea stone down to create a parking area. It was when he noted the tire tracks circling the cottage that he grew concerned.

Slamming the truck in park and cutting the engine, he left the meal in the cab and sprinted to her red front door. He banged on the door only once before he tested the knob. Every possible worst-case scenario crossed his mind while he waited for her to answer.

The doorknob turned at his will, allowing him to enter the dark cavernous cottage. But it shouldn't be like this. In all his years of entering the humble residence, never once had it felt this sad.

"Beth?" He called into the room. "It's me, Scott. I'm letting myself in."

Looking to the room on his right, he took in the rustic kitchen. Only discarded items on the table looked out of place. There was no Beth.

He then made his way to the room on the other side of the entrance. The overstuffed couch that had been a staple in the living room had been replaced by a daybed couch of sorts. A new rocker sat in the opposing corner. Scott scanned the room but found no sign of her.

"Beth? Are you here?" He asked as he made his way up the stairs to the loft. Her bed rested at the far end of the room, but the blankets were smooth and without any hint that it had been slept in.

Next, he checked outside, but like the cottage, she was nowhere to be found.

"Beth?" He called out one more time as he stood in the middle of the house with hands resting on his hips. Perplexed, he looked from the kitchen to the living room. "She has to be here, but where?" he muttered.

Movement came from the daybed that sat in the middle of the room facing the fireplace. It only took a few steps forward for him to see that what he thought was a mound of throw pillows and blankets was really Beth.

She laid there, curled into a ball with one of Gram's many afghans draped over her slender figure. A section of her long mahogany colored locks lay across her forehead. Her lips were parted as the steadiness of her breathing captured his attention. There was no restlessness or agitation—no business or confusion. She was at peace for a change, and he didn't want to disturb that.

Leaving her presence was also something he did not want to do, so he went back out to the truck to get the food. He put it in her refrigerator as quietly as possible so that they could share it when she woke. Noticing the randomness of the discarded items on the table and the sink full of dirty dishes, he glanced back into the living room to make sure she still rested and rolled up his sleeves.

Doubt pricked at his heart as he ran hot water into the sink. *You know how this might look, don't you? Maybe you should just leave her alone. She doesn't want your help.* Scott knew better though. The evidence of burn-out and even maybe depression surrounded him. Those were the moments that someone should invade on another's privacy. At least that was something his dad had told him years back.

He didn't hear the rustle of covers again for another hour. In that time had Scott washed and dried the dishes, swept and mopped the old wood floors, dusted some of her bookshelves, and even found time to relax in the rocking chair with some Tolkien. Glancing in her direction at the end of each page, Scott couldn't help but admire the woman.

With a stretch and a purring moan. He was blessed to see those eyes that he thought about often. *God, she is beautiful in so many ways.*

"Good afternoon, sleepy ferret. I was beginning to wonder when you would wake up."

Confusion crossed her face as she reached for her cell phone to see the time. "Oh, my goodness. I can't believe I slept that long. How long have you ... oh wait, fifteen missed calls and one text message?"

"You wouldn't answer your phone and I was worried. Sorry." Scott placed the book on the side table, got up and went to the kitchen, "Hungry? I brought dinner."

He could hear her bare-feet pad across the floor behind him. "What? You cooked, too?"

"I made a Thanksgiving feast and didn't want to eat it alone. So, I brought it over." He pulled out a chair for her, inviting her to have a seat. "I just need to warm it up."

"I can help," she declared as she made a move to stand.

"You just sit down and let me do this. You clearly needed the break."

"If you say so. Wait, where did everything go that I put on the table?" Beth sat up in the bed, rubbed her eyes and looked about the room. "And my dishes? Scott, how long have you been here?"

A smile spread across his face as he made quick work of putting things in pans. "Long enough to see how much you drool in your sleep."

Beth wiped at her face and he couldn't hold back the laughter. "I'm just kidding. You were a regular sleeping beauty."

She scoffed at his compliment but gave no reply.

When everything was edible again, he set the table using Gram's china and silver that she kept in the corner cupboard. As he placed each item on the table, Beth gave him a scolding look. A look that his mom would give dad when he used more dishes than necessary to make dinner. "Don't worry, little ferret, I will do the dishes again and I promise not to break a single dish."

"I sure hope so. It smells divine though. Where did you learn to cook a feast like this?"

Scott stopped what he was doing, a hot casserole dish still in his covered hands. "You are not the only one Gram taught to cook." He set the dish down and took a seat at the head of the table, beside Beth. Encasing her soft slender hand in his rough calloused one, he ran his thumb across her fingers. Thoughts swirled as his heart raced with the speed of a hundred stallions. There was so much he wanted to say to her, and judging from the look in her eyes, she had things to say as well. Now was not the time, so he bowed his head to pray.

They enjoyed the meal as they reminisced of their summers on the islands, clearly avoiding their last summer together. The one where their innocent friendship changed into something more. She was no longer Mr. and Mrs. Lewis' bubbly grand-daughter, but a stunning work of God's artful design. A work of art that even after more than a decade, he still could not have.

"What's on your mind?" Her quiet question pulled him from his thoughts.

"I'm not sure you are ready to know." Scott looked down at his plate, doing his best to keep it all in.

"What makes you say that? I can handle it. I think."

"That's it, you're unsure. Until you know what you want, I can't even begin to share with you what I think about almost every moment I don't see you." He knew he said too much, but it was out now and there was no taking it back.

When she didn't reply, Scott gave her a quick look and saw her eyes widen with understanding and her lips parted in awe. The longing to meet her lips with his own began to cloud his sensibilities, so he stood to clear the table. If he didn't look at her, maybe he wouldn't want to hold her.

For the second time, he ran hot water in the sink to prep for doing dishes. He turned it to the hottest setting possible, maybe the pain would make him forget how inviting her mouth was.

The scrape of the wooden chairs on the bare kitchen floor announced that she was done eating as well. The clattering of silverware and dirty, empty dishes filled the void that their words couldn't. Within minutes, she stood to his right with a towel in her hand. They worked in silence as Scott's thoughts taunted him. Visions of Beth, large with child, observing him pulling an over stuffed turkey from the oven as their closest friends gathered around the table. *She would be a wonderful mother.*

Once they'd washed and dried every dish and the table was wiped down, Scott stood on the back porch, hoping the sounds of the sea would clear his head. The sound usually helped calm him, and it almost did, but a steaming cup of coffee appeared before him. His senses heightened again knowing she was close.

Just as he was about to say something, his gaze landed on the Bronco in the backyard. The unusual way it was parked set off warning bells. Knowing how he found her when he arrived, worry squeezed his lungs.

"Beth, why is there a track around the cottage, and your truck parked like that?"

Silence answered him in all the wrong ways. *This can't be good.*

eth wasn't sure what had happened; forget about trying to explain it to Scott. Maybe someone could explain it to her. All she knew was that she couldn't stop. He would be furious as soon as she told him, and he would be dead set on being around her all the time until this mess was over. After his minor confession, she felt the weight of his feelings for her and with it came his protective nature. She didn't want that. At least, that was what she told herself, though watching him cook a meal and doing the dishes made her want to toss all her determination into the wind and let him in her heart.

"Beth, what happened?" His tone was softer, less commanding this time.

"I couldn't stop. My brakes were gone. I had to drive around the house until I began to slow down."

Anger flashed in his eyes. "Did you have new brake lines put in that thing before you drove down here?"

"Yes. Everything was tuned up, cleaned up, or beefed up to be able to haul the trailer."

Scott asked her to pop the hood so he could take a look.

Beth went around and opened the driver-side door, leaning

in to pull the hood latch. Scott lifted the hood, the movement pulling the sleeves tight around his arms and back. He proceeded to move wires and check different elements of the engine compartment. She wanted to offer to help but had no idea what he was looking for. He stopped and came around to the driver's side front wheel well. Words began to fill the air as he moved several feet away from the Bronco, unkind words about a certain mayor who had a fascination with her cottage.

"Scott, what is it?"

He marched back to the Bronco, fire raging in his expression. He tapped the wheel. "That should be connected."

She must have given him a confused look because Scott knelt down and held two hoses that were tucked behind the wheel. "There is a hole in your brake line."

"Did it get caught in something? Is it even possible? I honestly don't know what I am looking at. "

"The way it is notched out, someone had to physically get under there and do it. You have a big enough hole that you can lose fluid but not as rapidly as if it had been completely severed."

The gravity of what he was saying hit her in one fell swoop. The earth began to tilt under her, forcing her to the ground. "Who would do that?"

Scott asked a list of questions concerning where she'd been, who she saw, and suspicious behavior.

"People have been acting strange for weeks now. There has been a steady decline in patrons since that slow day on Hooper. I figured it was the holiday season, so I came home the other day ready to take the next few weeks off."

"What island were you on that day?"

"Elnora. You were there."

Scott took hold of her shoulders—urgency, determination, concern, and a bit of fear all radiated from him. She'd never witnessed fear in him, not even as kids. "Who did you see?"

"Some moms with their children, gossiping women sharing nasty things about me with each other, and before I left, Valerie was there with some guy."

"Had you ever seen the guy before?"

Fear wrapped its fingers around her, forcing her mute. Shaking her head was all she could offer.

"Could you describe him?"

"Um," she searched her memory for his face. "Dark every-thing—hair, eyes, clothes."

"And you saw him with Valerie?"

She confirmed with a nod. Her head was still reeling from his behavior.

"He got to her," Scott mumbled. He asked her more about the encounter with Valerie and Beth told him, not sure what he was getting at as she explained. And then the light bulb turned on.

"Scott, do you think Valerie and that man had something to do with the Bronco?"

He let go of her and turned away and paced the length of the Bronco and trailer while mumbling something inaudible. She needed to break the tension somehow because his erratic gesturing was beginning to freak her out just a bit. "You pace when you are processing, did you know that?" She couldn't help but tease him. "Do you know how to think standing still, Scotty boy?"

That got the response she desired as the tension left his face. Scott chuckled before he took a deep breath. "Let's go inside and we can talk."

Once in the living room, Beth took her place on the daybed couch as she moved pillows to make it look less like a bed. Scott sat next to her, but when his eyes began to shift around the space and his ears changed to a crimson color, she knew he wouldn't stay. He stood and moved to the rocking chair in the corner of the room.

"You find a man who respects you enough to put his desires on the

back burner and loves you enough to never put you in a compromising situation. That's the kind of man you join forces with for life," Gram had told her after a bad break-up. Scott's gallant behavior now, and over the last several weeks, reflected that of the kind of man Gram spoke of. She just wasn't ready to deal with that level of love and affection.

Scott leaned forward, placing his elbows on his legs, and he cupped his head in hands and rubbed them over his face. "So, after the fire, I went over to Savannah. I have some friends who are detectives with the police department. They weren't sure how much of a case there was but said they would look into it. Beth, I have to call them over to see this."

Beth contemplated her options. She could tell him not to bother but what if this continued? What if next time more than just her bank account suffered? That was something she didn't want to go through.

"Okay, call them."

The shock on his face brought a smile to her heart. "You're not mad I talked to them without you? I mean, I thought..."

"Scott, it's fine. I'm glad you went. Something needs to be done. Please call them."

She watched him as he stepped out onto the back deck. His willingness to take charge, not of her life but on her behalf, touched her in a way she'd never felt before. He was willing to fight for her, to protect her from evil. Besides Daddy and Gram, no one had ever protected her.

Maybe that is what love looks like.

The thought brought tears to her eyes and a warmth in her heart. She did have people who loved her and cared about her well-being. More people than just Gram.

Beth got up and went to the kitchen, and the feeling of completeness from earlier filled her once again. Scott provided a delicious meal. He stood guard in the corner of her living room and watched over her as she slept. Never once did he make an advance on her, cheapen her existence, or tell her she was doing everything wrong. His quiet nature was a testament to his constant study of the Word and spending time in prayer. He still had a stinker streak, but his actions were reverent of all of God's creation, including her.

"That's great, Blake. I'll see you tomorrow. Hey, thanks a lot." Scott ended the call as he walked in the door. He hadn't looked at her yet; he was typing something into his phone, so she took a moment to admire him. The comfort of their long-time friendship only deepened the desire to have him near.

Forever? Gram's voice asked in her head. Beth could only smile.

"So, my friends will be here tomorrow to investigate. I encouraged them to bring their families to keep it low key. Keep suspicion at bay and all."

"That could be fun, but how would that work? Two families who are not from Merriweather walking around the island is kind of conspicuous. Don't you think?"

"Well, not tomorrow."

Confused at his comment, she asked, "What's tomorrow?"

"I guess you haven't heard. Every year, for as long as I can remember, Merriweather Island throws one amazing Christmas kick-off party. Tomorrow, residents will decorate their three-wheelers, golf carts, and lawn mowers with Christmas lights and drive around the island in a parade. At the end of the parade, there is a tree lighting down at the docks.

"Anyway, people come from all over the islands for this so they will blend in."

As she listened to him describe the fun, a switch flipped inside, turning on all the lights and illuminating the dark places. Excitement bubbled up, and she knew exactly what must happen to turn the gloom and sadness into joy.

"Then I have work to do tonight." Beth couldn't contain the

smile as the giddiness continued to build. "Would you like to be my little helper, Scotty boy?"

Scott's chuckle filled the room as he took her hand in his. "What did you have in mind, Miss Ferret?"

"Christmas cookies, of course!"

21

*I*n a fit of laughter, Scott and Beth sank to the baking flour covered floor. Never had he had so much fun baking Christmas cookies. Flour covered every surface of the kitchen, as well as their hair and clothes. The room was white as snow from their flour fight and, for the first time in a couple of years, the gloom had been lifted from his heart.

Beth's shoulder pressed into his own as they laughed until they hurt at their antics.

"Oh, my goodness, Scott, laughing has never hurt my stomach this much."

"I know what you mean. I'm not too sure we can get up, let alone clean up the mess."

Scott let his gaze scan across the room, calculating how many hours it would take to remove the mess they'd made. At last he caught a glimpse of white streaks of flour that high-lighted her hair and he couldn't help but admire beautifully disheveled features.

She looked up at him at that moment, causing his heart to pause mid beat. Her eyes sparkled with joy and her smile shone like a radiant light. He reached over to wipe away the flour that dusted the bridge of her nose. Longing for more filled his heart. It would take nothing to wrap her in his arms and hold her until time stopped.

Her hand raised to his to check what he was wiping away. "You have flour on your nose."

"Thanks."

Her gaze pierced his. If he were to lean in just a little, a kiss would be the perfect way to end this fight.

Beth turned her attention to the rest of the room, breaking the current that was surging between them. "Look at this place," she sprang up from the floor before he regained his bearings.

He leaned forward and placed his palms on the floor to better stabilize himself as he rose. The dampness of his hands combined with the powdery substance only created a paste in his palms. The sensation distracted him from any romantic intentions he might have had.

After wiping his hands on the towel that hung at his waist, he asked, "Do we bake more or clean?"

Beth walked to the closet in the kitchen and produced a broom and dustpan. She marched back to him, holding the items out for him to take. "You clean, I bake."

"As you wish."

She gave him a knowing smile. "You can't use movie lines like that right now."

He leaned against the counter, placing his hands on the edge. He couldn't help but tease her. She was too cute with flour still clinging to her hair and face. "And why not, may I ask?"

The smile disappeared and the broom and dustpan in her hands hung at her side. "Scott, please don't look at me that way."

She set the items against the table, turned her back to him and reached for the bowl containing what was left of the cookie dough. He watched as she worked the dough on the countertop, not at all surprised by her statement. Something spooked her.

There was a burning question that needed to be answered

before he could decide on what to do next. He would give her a minute though, because he needed to process his thoughts after all the fun and laughter they'd shared together.

Once he'd swept the last speck of flour and she placed the last of the cookies on the cooling rack, they sat down at the kitchen table with a few leftovers from their holiday meal and cups of coffee. They ate in silence as he mulled over the things he wanted to say. When the tension grew to an unbearable level, he knew that it was time to have that conversation.

He twisted the coffee cup between his hands as he contemplated how to begin. The choice of words that he used would be paramount.

Just share your heart.

"Beth," he fought to keep his hands on the cup, "do you know that I love you?"

"Well, of course you do. Friends love each other." The pitch of her voice hinted at some over-exaggeration.

"If it only were simple." He reached over and engulfed her hand that rested on her coffee mug. "It's not, though. It is something much bigger."

He hoped understanding set in.

"I wish, I wish I could give you what it is that you're looking for. That I can be the girl you once knew. But I can't be that for you."

He would play along. "And why would you say that?"

"You haven't seen me in a decade, for starters. So much has happened to shape the person I am now, but you haven't even begun to get to know her."

"Why is that?"

Silence filled the room as he waited for her answer. He could only pray that she would open up. That she would be honest with him and herself.

"Because I won't let you see her. Honestly, I don't even know who she is."

Scott let her words, and the meaning behind them, soak in. She made a valid point, and shame beat at his chest for not even trying to get to know the woman she was now.

"I see what you're saying, and I apologize for not trying harder. You're right. I looked at you differently on that ferry the first day when I thought you were just another woman with a familiar golden glint in her eye. When I found out it was you, that lens changed, and I did look at you like I did when we were teenagers.

"Can I ask you another question?" She only gave a nod. "Can we figure this out together?"

He was willing to wait for as long as it would take for her to discover the treasure that she was. No, he might not see her as the woman that she is today. He saw her as a child of God and that was more important than any other perception.

"Why would you even want to? I'm a mess. The last few months hold plenty of evidence to that."

The despondent look on her face ignited a war with his emotions. Anger flared over the fact that someone must have beat her down to this level that she didn't find herself worthy of love. Yet, compassion for her wounded heart flowed through him and he wanted nothing more than to help.

"Yes, you have been a little...um, unhinged but..."

"Are you saying I am crazy?" The pitch of her voice heightened, throwing him a warning. He did not start out right.

"No! I'm sorry, that didn't come out right. But let me finish, please. Yes, you have been a little off lately. Who wouldn't be? You have been through some major life changes and I understand that. I still want to be here, with you."

Her body language didn't show any understanding of what he was trying to convey, and it frustrated him. Scott stood from the table and took his cup and plate to the sink. A glance at the clock on the wall indicated the late hour, and he had a lot of work to do before tomorrow afternoon. But he couldn't leave without asking her one more thing.

"I don't know your full story; I don't know who has hurt you. I don't even know the extent of your self-loathing, but I have seen the tenderness that you still possess in the way that you serve our community. I see your longing to be loved, and not just by a man." She sat rigid with her back to him. Not sure what else to say to help her see, he ran his fingers through his hair and let out a huff. "Look, we're tired and stressed, so I'm just gonna go but I want you to know one thing. I'm not blind, Beth, but I'm not pushy either, despite the desire to kiss you on a daily basis. All I am asking is that you give me a chance to get to know the woman you have become."

When she didn't give a reply, he went to her, placed his hand on her shoulder and kissed the top of her head. He went to the door and put his jacket on, every step feeling like a mile between them. He hated leaving things like this, but maybe she needed time to think.

Scott looked back at her before walking out the door. She sat alone at the table with flour still in hair and the image made him smile. *I still love her, Lord. Help me figure this out.*

Journal Entry
November 26th
  I feel like I've been hit by a hurricane. The emotional highs and lows of today have played a wicked game on me.
  I felt the loss of Gram intensely this morning, so instead of facing it, I closed the curtains and decided to sleep the day away. I'm glad I still chose to take a shower or else Scott would've been in for the shock of his life when he walked in the door. I can't imagine what Scott's thoughts were when he first saw the disheveled state of my kitchen.

But he would never let on how scared he was. I must say, making cookies for tomorrow was fun.

Then he had to ruin it. He had to ask tough questions that I was not ready to answer. Shoot, I don't even know the answers myself. Being straightforward with him was the only thing I knew to do. It's clear he is willing to wait, but am I willing to let him?

Beth

22

"Well, don't you look bright-eyed and bushy-tailed. Rough night?" Scott asked as Beth approached him on the pier. His disheveled hair melted into his day and a half beard. His green plaid flannel shirt, jeans that fit just snug enough, and a burnt orange puffy vest gave him a look that fit in more with the men in Michigan.

The icing on the cake, and the part that left her pulse racing, was the travel coffee cups he held in his hands. *Be still my heart.*

Scott gave her a tentative glance. "I have a peace offering."

"Not that you need one."

"Well, that gives me hope," he mumbled. "Are you still mad from last night?"

That was the question of the morning. She'd spent most of the night rolling his words around while she tossed and turned. When the sun started to peek its light into her bedroom window, she decided not to fight it anymore. The man loved her; she knew it. She didn't need to fight it.

"I was never mad. At least I shouldn't have been. I'm sorry for giving you that impression." She wanted to say more, but uncertainty prevented that.

Be honest.

Being honest hurt. It wasn't pleasant sometimes, but she knew it was necessary to make any relationship work.

"I'm scared, okay. Like you said, everything has changed, and that terrifies me."

Scott nodded and gave her that smile she loved. "Okay. I can work with that."

Letting the matter drop, Scott extended the two cups he held. "We have hazelnut—one that is dark as the night and one that is blonde and doctored. Take your pick."

"You don't leave much of a choice, Scotty boy," she teased. "You know I don't drink black coffee." He extended the correct cup and held the other closer to his chest. "Thank you."

"I'm glad you chose that one," he lifted the other cup. "This one is half gone already." His playfulness pulled at her heart. He really was the full package.

Love will find you when you least expect, sugar. You may not even want it or be looking for it, but then it will show up on your front door, begging to come in. Let it in, Gram once told her. Beth wondered if she had been talking of Scott all along. How could she deny him?

What would it hurt?

When she took the warm cup, she let its heat chase away the chill in her hands. They stood, side by side, along the railing as they watched the ocean waves crash against the coast. A cluster of seagulls flew overhead. They landed not far away, their demands for scraps piercing the air. A fish jumped nearby and sent the crazy white birds into a frantic tizzy.

She and Scott laughed at the spectacle as they both shifted their bodies to stand closer together. The moment their arms touched, a quivering within her stuttered her breath as she struggled to inhale. She longed to loop her arm through his and snuggle in tight to his side while they waited for the ferry to arrive with his friends.

Let yourself go; let him in, sugar, Gram's voice commanded.

"I have a penny if you want to tell me what you're thinking," Scott held a copper coin between his finger and thumb out in front of her, giving her a coaxing grin.

She could only smile at his joke for fear that her words would come out wrong.

"No? Okay then," he took the coin and put it back in his pocket.

Just give in already, she scolded herself. The man served up his heart on her kitchen table last night and left without a reply from her. She needed to give him some indication of her thoughts since then. To let him know that she could think of nothing else but him over the last twelve hours, not to mention several times a day since she arrived.

Her heart hammered in her chest as she slid her right hand between his left arm and his torso, hooking her arm with his, and resting her head on his bicep. She felt his chest expand and hold before he released the breath. With great anticipation, she waited for him to remark on her action or ask a question, but minutes went by without a word. When the ferry came into view and she caught sight of two men waving at them from the lower deck, she knew their moment was coming to an end.

"I have so much I want to say," Scott began.

"But we don't have the time right now. Just let it be."

"I can try," he gave her a wink as her arm slipped from his protective hold, and he walked to the gate to meet his friends.

Scott hadn't told her much about the brothers, so when they approached with their wives and little ones, she was caught off guard. The only difference in the pair was their clothing. "How do their wives tell them apart?" she muttered to herself. The closer they got, though, she began to see the small things that made each man unique and identifiable.

"Beth, I would like you to meet Blake." She noted the graying at the temples and the slightly crooked nose. "And this is Jacob."

He sported a nice tan, and a head of hair that was unmarred by silver streaks.

She held out her hand to greet them. "Welcome to Merriweather Island."

"And these sainted women are their wives. Tina." Her fire red locks were cropped short and her porcelain skin glimmered. She hung on the arm of the first brother so she could safely assume she was his wife. On her hip rested a beautiful baby boy with a complexion like his dad's but hair like his mother's. A shot of longing pierced her heart when Blake looked down at his wife and son with adoration in his eyes. What would it be like to have a little someone in her life that was the perfect combination of herself and his daddy? She tossed a quick glance at Scott and her cheeks warmed.

"This is, you'll like this," Scott called to Beth, "Elizabeth, or Liz for short." She and the dark auburn-haired woman shared the same name. This brought a smile to Beth's face. The woman touched her belly, bringing attention to the coming arrival.

"Who currently looks like a lazy walrus," Liz proclaimed.

Beth shook the woman's hand. "You look radiant."

Another pain shot through Beth, but she kept her smile in place. She never thought of wanting children of her own until now. *And it only took one conversation with Scott.*

"Shall we head to Beth's?" Scott asked the detective brothers.

"Yes. I want to get this over with so that we can enjoy the holiday weekend," Tina commanded with a glare at her husband.

"Actually, can you give us a tour, Scott? Show us some key locations." Beth watched as he gave Scott a look that she didn't understand but Scott did.

"Sure." Scott reached in his pocket and handed the keys to his truck to Beth. "Can I trust you not to scratch it?"

Beth put a hand on her hip and leaned to one side, arching an eyebrow at the absurdity of his question.

141

"I will take that as a yes. I'll put your bike in the back. You guys can walk, right?"

As the group walked toward the truck, Beth leaned closer to Scott. "Why didn't they just land in Breakers from Mimosa and drive their cars? It's closer to the cottage and a little faster."

Scott bowed his head low so only she could hear him. "You would deny me the honor of your arm hooked with mine, even for a few moments?" She felt a blush bloom again and refused to answer. Scott only chuckled, "I'm not sure. Maybe it is for the experience. They've never been out here before."

"Makes sense. What do I do with the wives and the little one? I've never hosted before."

"Wow them with your cooking skills, maybe? I have a load of groceries in the back seat of the truck. I thought it only fair that I provide the food to entertain with since I did invite them over."

"I think I can do that," she gave him a look. "I am more than what I can cook, though."

"I know that all too well."

"Would you look at them? It's like they're in love or something. Ow!" Jacob howled from behind them. Beth looked back to see Liz give her husband a good pinch.

Beth took a step away; not sure she liked the attention.

"Look at what you did. You embarrassed her, and you just met her. You big oaf," Tina reprimanded her brother-in-law a little louder than necessary.

"Like you're not embarrassing them now," he bit back.

Beth couldn't help but laugh at the antics between them. That is until she realized she would never have something like that with her in-laws. Her brothers-in-law were stuffy and money hungry. They barely interacted with their own families, let alone her.

"How long is the drive?" Tina asked as she gestured towards

her child. Clearly, they had forgotten something in the planning.

"Can't you just hold onto him, honey?" Blake asked his wife.

"Well, it's not ideal but we can try. I guess maybe we should've driven. That way we would have had a car seat."

"Give me one second. You'd be amazed at what people leave behind on the ferries." Scott darted away from the group and made his way to the main office. He returned minutes later with his ninety-watt smile glistening in the morning sun and a baby seat in his arms. "Will this work?"

"Well, look at you, Mr. Hero-of-the-Moment. Are you showing off for your new girlfriend?" Jacob asked in a mocking tone.

"You hush. You used to be the same way." Liz's irritation with her husband's jokes was clearly reaching its tipping point.

"Oh, we're just friends," Beth interjected.

She looked to Scott to see if he heard her. Confusion replaced his smile and shame tore through her heart. She did that to him.

Did she dare confess publicly what she hadn't even spoken to him about? *You know you want to.*

"For now, at least."

That wiped the confused look from his face and earned her a nod.

Beth couldn't help but feel proud when the compliments on her "cute little cottage" began. She helped Liz out of Scott's oversized truck while Tina unhooked her little boy.

Beth, Liz, and Tina walked the perimeter of the cottage, talking about flowers and how life was on the island compared to the cold north.

"I will admit, it is strange seeing you all dressed in sweaters and boots in this sixty-degree weather when in Michigan, we're walking around with t-shirts or lightweight sweaters or jackets. When I talked to my dad this morning, he said that it was only forty degrees up there today. Snow will be coming over the weekend."

"Oh, you can forget about snow down here. I know when I moved down here from Boston, I missed the snow that first Christmas. Not so much now," Tina informed her.

"You're from Boston? I didn't know that."

"Scott didn't tell you? Liz and her son are from there as well as Colorado."

"Wait," news that there was another child jarred Beth. "Where is your son? He would have been welcome."

"Beth, that is kind of you." Liz displayed a sudden sadness. "He would rather spend time with his girlfriend and her family."

"How old is he?"

"He is sixteen now. I feel like I am about to lose one family member while God blesses me with another." Liz continued to rub her rounded stomach. "I hate to ask, but Scott said something about you being a great cook."

They all laughed. The little tyke included.

"Are you saying you're hungry?" Tina asked.

"I can definitely make some breakfast. Let's see what Scott picked up and pray it is worthy of consumption."

23

"$\mathcal{I}$t has been way too long since I have ridden a bike," a winded Jacob declared as they crested the hill in front of Beth's cottage.

The sight of it brought a smile to Scott's face. He liked the freedom of his houseboat, but whether it was the feel of the place, fond memories, or Beth, the cottage felt like home.

He'd left so quickly last night that he hadn't given Beth a chance to turn him down. He figured that she needed time to think about what he said. Today, it seemed to have worked, too.

She had avoided his touch or jumped every time their fingers grazed before, so for her to loop her arm through his and nestle in was clearly a sign that she was willing to let him in. He wanted to talk about it then and there, but she made it clear that she wasn't ready yet. *That was okay by him. Just being with her was more than enough.*

Blake kicked off the teasing with, "Okay, lover boy, what has you all, all, oh…I don't know what to call it?"

Jacob joined in his brother's torment. "Flaky? Is that the word you're looking for?"

"Jake, how does your wife tolerate you?" Scott asked as

straight-faced as possible. "Blake, when did he turn out like this? He used to be such a nice guy."

"Hey, I've always been a bit of a stinker, but I am serious when it is necessary." Jacob glanced between Blake and Scott. "Like now. Show me this Bronco."

Once they parked the bikes on the side of the cottage, Scott led them to the back of the cottage. He hoped that they could pick up a fingerprint or something to offer as evidence. Maybe then they could link the culprit that gouged the line to the mayor.

A long whistle pierced the air, scattering the birds that liked to hide out in the long grass lining the cliff.

"That's a nice ride. Who did the work?"

"Someone up in Michigan did it for her. The guy did a primo job if you ask me."

The guys circled the vehicle, marveling at the workmanship, as if it were a shrine. From inside, Scott could hear feminine laughter, and a piece of him longed to be inside to be close to her.

Slow down. She is just now warming up to you.

"Are you mooning over her again? You have got it bad, man," Blake slapped him on the shoulder, jarring him from his thoughts.

"I'm sorry, guys. Maybe just a little."

"Maybe just a lot. What's the deal?"

"I just got her to finally be willing to open up about things. She is as tight as a bank vault when it comes to some things. And don't even get me started on her family. But how about you tell me what to do to keep her safe?"

"You can't, Scott," Jacob's somber tone reflected the other side of the man. "You have to trust God to keep her safe. Being with her twenty-four seven is not an option."

"No, it isn't. She might hurt me if I try." He couldn't help but chuckle. "You should see some of the knives that woman uses."

Nervous chuckles hung in the air. "So, back to the Bronco? What do you need?"

"We need to go in there and talk to her," Jacob informed him. "But first, talk to me about what you found on this beautiful Bronco."

Scott took them to the driver's side of the vehicle and showed him what he found. Jacob knelt down to get a better look at the line. "I don't see how it could have gotten caught on anything. I'll test for prints. I am guessing yours are on here."

"Yes." Scott looked over to Blake to say something but saw him writing something in his little notebook.

"Has it rained out here since this happened?" Blake asked him.

"Not in the last week."

"While he checks that, tell me about this mayor and your involvement with the man."

Scott knew he had told them before, but it was necessary. He began to tell him everything he knew about the mayor, his dealings, his barely legal behavior and practices, and the employee abuse he had witnessed.

Blake hemmed and hawed as he wrote everything down. He then slapped the notebook shut and slid the pen in its place. He looked around at the tire tracks that encircled the cottage. Scott painfully waited for him to say something, anything, and could only surmise that it was a tactic.

As Jacob reassembled his pocket evidence kit, he gave his findings. "Okay, I could only pick up a couple of prints. When we get inside, I'll get a sample of yours as something to compare it to."

"Scott, I'm going to tell you something that you won't want to hear, but I think it needs to be said. Unless we have a print on that hose that is not yours that belongs to someone that we can tie back to Mr. Ainsley, she doesn't have a case. It could look like you did it. Once I open an investigation, I can't control

147

what direction it takes. Are you willing to deal with the possibility that this all could point to you?" Blake's somber look only stressed how serious this situation was.

Of all the scenarios, that was one he had never thought of. He could be implicated in this and there would be nothing to argue in his defense besides an alibi.

"Unless she has some information that can save you," Jacob stated.

Scott's head began to pound at what he was implying. "She was there when I found the line."

Black gave him a stern look. "Was she with you when it happened?"

"Well, no."

Jacob shook his head. "I have to ask, Scott. Where were you that day?"

Scott searched his memory while attempting to push down the anger brewing. There had to be a reason for this kind of questioning. "I was doing my job on the ferry all day."

Blake gave a nod while he opened his book again and began to write. "The other day you said you were on Elnora."

"I was. One of the water taxi drivers called in and they needed someone to drive the boat. I did a shift while a fill-in took a break." Scott's heart dropped. "I saw her truck there and went over to say hello, but I was only there for a couple minutes."

Blake closed the book and gave Scott a pat on the back. "That will do. Just breathe, man. We had to ask."

Scott let out a heavy breath. "I knew that in my head, but, wow, it was intense as I thought about how this could look."

Jacob chimed in, "Don't sweat it. Now let's go pester the girls."

Scott guided them to the back door, the weight of everything sitting heavy on his shoulders. He had only just connected with

Beth and being away from her at such a crucial time was not something he was looking forward to.

He opened the French doors and they were greeted with the most beautiful collection of smiles and the sounds of laughter. Yeah, falling for Beth turned him into a sap, but he didn't care. He knew what he felt in his heart and nothing would deter him.

"Sounds like you ladies are having too much fun in here. Wait, what do I smell?" Scott knew that their guests were in for quite a treat at the scent of nutmeg, vanilla, and sausage.

"I made Gram's best comfort food and she always had the makings for it available around the holidays. If you put in a pinch too much sugar, it's a dessert. Otherwise it's perfect for breakfast. Gentleman, have a seat."

He went to Beth while the other two went and kissed their wives. The idea was nice, but he would keep that to himself.

Placing a hand on the small of her back, he whispered, "You made Gram's French toast, didn't you? You sure know how to get my attention."

Beth cleared her throat as her neck and ears turned a rosy shade of pink. "How about you get mine and pour your friends some coffee?" she murmured as she looked at him over her shoulder with an impish grin.

"Oh, little ferret, I think I have your attention." He went for it, feeling light as air, and gave her a peck on the cheek.

He darted out of her reach laughing like a little kid, before she slapped him with the spatula. There was no denying the attraction any longer and he was glad of it. It was definitely Beth that made the cottage feel like home and this was right where he wanted to be. So, he wouldn't push her too hard, but he didn't see the harm in the occasional, playful peck. The smile she gave him as she swung at him told him she didn't mind either.

"Family, food, and fun - that's what life is about, Scotty. Always surround yourself with those things," Gram had told him once

during a cooking lesson. Scott couldn't help but feel like this was exactly what she meant. It didn't matter if the people were related; as long as you loved one another like family should, then you were family.

"So, Beth, tell me about your little encounter." Blake broke into the laughter with the mood killing request as he cut away at the food on his plate.

Without missing a beat, she began to relay to him not just the incident that resulted in her turning the yard into a dirt track, but details of the fire as well.

"Did you recognize the man with this Valerie woman?" he asked.

Without hesitation, Beth said, "No, I've never seen him before."

"Well, Scott, that may have just saved your sorry backside," Blake informed them.

Beth gave a curious look at all three men. The concern for him was clear as the sky outside. He took her hand. "They say that if we don't play our cards right, this could come back around and bite me. There is not enough definitive evidence to keep me in the clear."

A determined look flashed and she turned to him. "Well, then I guess we have to keep you on the right side of the law."

After breakfast, the guys rode the rented bicycles back to the pier while Beth drove Tina, Liz, and the baby in Scott's truck. To avoid any more ribbing by his friends, he contained the excitement of being able to spend the day with the most important people in his life.

A carnival of sorts had been set up along Madeline Lane. Games, rides, fun food vendors all enticed people to come to their booths for a good time. Scott glanced at Beth to see her response, knowing she was missing out on an opportunity to get her business known. Her face confirmed his concern. She wanted to be here working, not acting as a spectator.

"Maybe you can have a spot for next year," he leaned in and remarked.

"Oh, it's okay. Really, it is. I'm just being reminded that sometimes we have to slow down to appreciate what is around us."

"Sounds like something Gram would say.."

"You would be right."

"One never knows what one is missing if one is always running."

They walked a while longer watching the Andrews enjoy the festivities as the four adults acted goofy for the little one. The comical image prompted a deep longing for the same thing, some day.

"Kind of fun to watch them interact together, isn't it?" he asked her.

"It's sweet. They are making fools of themselves for a two-year-old who won't remember."

"I guess having children gives the parents the permission to act like kids again." Beth only nodded in agreement. "I can hear the gears turning, Beth. Want to tell me what has you thinking so hard and not having fun?"

She let out a heavy sigh and took hold of his hand. No words, just like earlier.

He didn't think much of it the first time, but now he wondered at the actions. He'd heard it said that the way we act and the things we do speak to the true character of a person. With Beth, he only saw insecurity in the way she held his hand or arm but refused to talk. What did that imply about how well he knew her?

"A penny for your thoughts?" she asked this time.

Two can play this game. He lifted their entwined hands and only pointed to them. No words.

She gave him a sidelong glance. "Are you okay with this?"

His only response was a partial nod because he wasn't

completely okay with it. He wanted to hear her voice, to talk with her.

She let out a small giggle. "You really hate not talking, don't you? Can't you just enjoy being together without words?"

Scott stopped in the middle of the street forcing her to stop and turn to him. Her hair swept across her face with the gentle breeze as her eyes danced in the sunlight.

"Not when you push me away one day and hold my hand the next. No, I don't like the quiet between us. I want to know your thoughts. I'm not a mind reader, Beth."

She looked around at the people mingling about until she found what she was looking for. With a jerk of his arm, she pulled him to an alleyway between two houses.

In a little corner, she pulled him out of the view of the street. Her chest rose and fell with each breath. He watched her pulse beating in her slender neck. A neck he longed to...no, he couldn't let himself think of it. He told her he wanted to get to know the woman who she claimed was different from the girl he knew. It was a promise he wanted to keep, but the growing desire to hold her in his arms as he showered her with kisses was becoming more than he could handle.

Not able to take the silence, he urged, "Beth, talk to me." His voice coming out a little stronger than he intended.

Tears pooled in her eyes and they nearly broke his resolve. "Oh, honey," he softened. "What is it? I told you I'm here for you. What could you—"

She slid her hand up his arm until it hooked around his neck, and with a force he didn't think she possessed, she pulled him to her. Their lips met with an eagerness he didn't think she possessed. She tasted of French toast and sea air, and like any strong gale, she sent his head spinning. Wrapping one arm around her, he cupped her face with his other hand, slowing the kiss to a less heated and desperate level. Beth molded into his embrace, solidifying what he had known all along.

We belong together.

He still didn't know what she was thinking, but he was getting a pretty good idea.

Journal Entry
   November 27ᵗʰ
   I kissed Scott!!!!

winkle lights danced, children laughed, friends reconnected, venders called out, bells pierced the air, and one heated kiss highlighted her first Christmas season kick-off on Merriweather Island. And the kiss may have been the most life-changing event.

When Scott took her back to the cottage after seeing the Andrews families off at the pier, she wondered if he would want to talk about what happened. Instead, like the gentleman he was, he walked her to the door, kissed her cheek, and left. No words, no request for a repeat of earlier, just a simple good-bye. It only made things clearer to her that letting Scott into her life would be good.

Sitting up in her bed, sinking back into her pillows, Beth reached for her Bible and turned to the day's reading. The verses leapt right off the page and into her heart. They reminded her that God is love, and when we live a life in Christ, God and His love are always with her. It also stated that God's love is perfect and that there is no fear in His love because fear is judgment and His love only corrects in grace.

After the reading, she pushed play on her music app, and

began her stretches to warm up her body. As she went through the motions, the verses continued to play in her head. She was a child of God and He loved her. There was nothing to fear.

Then a new revelation came as she was in mid-stretch. *If you are open with Scott, there will be nothing to fear. He is a believer as well, which means he strives to love like God loves.*

Beth collapsed on her mat, letting the words of the scripture and the thoughts on Scott pour over her. He wasn't going to judge her if she opened up to him. All he wanted to do was know the woman she had become. Of course, she was trying to figure that out for herself.

She decided then that it was time to be transparent. He deserved it after all she put him through over the last five months.

Beth dug through her comforter that sat on the bed in a mess of white. When at last she found her cell phone, she sent Scott a text.

DINNER AT THE COTTAGE TONIGHT? IT IS TIME TO TALK.

I'LL BE THERE. 4:00?

A giddy nervousness bubbled up inside

PERFECT.

After she cleaned up, she poured herself a cup of coffee from her French press and hoisted herself up on the countertop. Bringing the cup to her lips, she could hear Gram scolding her. The thought made her smile.

Beth went over all the jumbled thoughts and attempted to sort through her feelings, all so she could give Scott a coherent explanation. Things just didn't make sense.

After a cup and a half of coffee with still no logical reasoning, she decided to ride her bike to Madeline Lane and see what she could find at the market to make tonight. A new creation was brewing and making Scott her guinea pig was always fun.

Once she stepped outside, the chill in the air sent her running back inside for her knit cardigan sweater. Just the simple change in the temperatures made it feel more like Christmas to her.

She rode past some palm trees and sea gulls, sand hills and sea grass, humming the last song she heard on her worship mix. There wasn't a care that kept her from soaking in all the beauty around her. The longer she rode, the more peace infused into her mind and in her heart. She knew that the decisions she made were the right ones and could only trust that this night of transparency would prove to be the right thing as well.

Peddling past the pier, she slowed her speed, hoping to catch a glimpse of him. If he saw her watching him, she would give him a wave and maybe blow him a kiss. *That's corny, Beth.* No matter how she did it, she would make sure he knew she was thinking about him and excited to see him tonight. Disappointment dashed her hopes when there was no sign of him.

"Watch out!" someone shouted, shaking her from her thoughts. She shifted her focus ahead of her in time to see a leopard print clad woman that could only be Valerie, yelling and waving her arms.

"Sorry," Beth said as she rode past. It wasn't like Valerie was about to get hit or anything. Beth found her standing in the grass with plenty of distance to know that she wouldn't hit the woman.

Banner's Market was abuzz with frenzied shoppers moving about. If Beth didn't know any better, she would think they were preparing for a snowstorm. Carts were packed with water jugs, bread, milk, and eggs. Finally seeing a friendly face, she walked up to Granny Mae in the produce aisle.

"Good morning, Granny Mae. How are you today?"

The woman turned to her, fear flashing in her eyes. "It's just terrible, dear. Haven't you heard? You mustn't have; you look too happy."

"Hear what, Granny?"

"The cargo boat that brings food to the island went up in

flames last night. They said it would take two weeks, if not more to get another shipment out here. That is unless we go to the mainland ourselves. Some of us can't do that."

Beth could then understand the reason for panic. She scanned the collection of customers and noted only a handful of young people. She didn't mind going to Savannah to stock up, but these people couldn't. Then a thought struck.

"What about Scott?"

"Oh, honey, it was one of his." The old woman put her knotted hand on Beth's arm. "He didn't tell you?"

"No, and I just talked with him." The worry etched itself on the woman's face and the only thing Beth could think to do was put an arm around her. "Just try to relax, Granny. We will get this figured out."

Beth picked up as few items as possible in order to save enough for others. Her pantry, refrigerator, and freezer were stocked. She shuffled through check out, wondering why Scott didn't say anything, as well as worrying about how to fix the brake line on the Bronco so she could help. She had the means, just not the parts.

Before pushing off on the bike, she placed her Bluetooth device in her ear and asked her phone to call Scott.

"Yeah?"

"Scott?"

"Oh, sorry, Beth. I didn't look at the caller ID. I take it you heard?"

"I did. In Banner's Market. The place is in a tizzy right now. Why didn't you tell me? We can postpone tonight." Not that she wanted to.

"No! No, I don't want to reschedule. I want to spend time with you, and after the day I'm having, it is the best place to be."

She sighed aloud. He wanted to spend time with her. How could she not love that? "Tell you what, I have ideas to help. We will talk tonight. Will I still see you at four?"

157

"I could use ideas. Thank you, Beth."

"Hey, it's what community does. I'll see you then."

The next four hours seemed to stretch out to eight hours as Beth monitored the clock while making her version of chicken and dumplings. She made the stew part, but she would have to wait to drop the dumplings. If she put them in too soon, they would become overcooked.

Just as she reached to turn off the burner, a knock sounded on the front door. She turned the burner down and went to welcome Scott.

Nerves twisted and turned in her stomach as she approached the door. There was so much to talk about, but she needed to remember that he just had possibly one of the worst days of his business's existence.

She rose on her toes to look through the window to make sure it was him before she opened the door. There were too many unusual things happening lately for her liking.

"It's me, Beth," she heard him call out from the other side of the door.

Beth took a deep inhale of breath, doing her best to calm herself before she opened the door. She didn't want to seem too eager.

"Are you going to open the door, ferret? It's cold out here," he begged.

She greeted him with as disapproving a look as possible, while struggling not to laugh at the sad face that greeted her. "Oh, you baby. Come on in. I would hate to see you turn into an ice cube."

"No joke, it's cold out there. Did you order this weather?" He shook out of his vest.

"Oh no, I was enjoying the heat." She took the vest from him and their hands grazed, sending delightful shivers up her arm.

Scott rubbed his hands together while his eyes roved over the kitchen. "It smells delicious in here. What have you been making?" He asked as he wandered to the stove and lifted the lid. "Wow, that smells…Oh, please tell me it's ready."

Beth couldn't help but laugh at his silliness. He was begging to eat without actually begging, and it was adorable.

"I am making chicken and dumplings, but I was waiting to drop the dumplings until you got here so they were perfect."

Scott moved to the side. "Well, don't let me get in your way, darlin'. Is there anything I can do?"

"Setting the table would be helpful," she directed.

Scott whistled a Christmas tune, giving it some unfamiliar flair that only added to the beauty of the song. "Well, that's a talent I didn't know you possessed."

"Thank you. My dad taught me when I was a kid."

Fifteen minutes later the dumplings were perfectly cooked. When Beth turned to put the pot on the table, she was greeted with an enchanting display of wildflowers, candles, her fancy glasses, and Gram's fine china.

"Oh, Scott! It's beautiful. I feel bad for making something so simple. This is French cuisine worthy."

"Your Gram always said to serve a meal on your best dishes when you were with someone you care about." The love in his eyes as he came around the table to take the heavy pot from her hands made her knees grow weak.

Oh, he is a keeper, sugar.

"Yes, I believe I heard her say it a time or two as well. Thank you for thinking of it."

He placed the pot on the little trivet in the middle of the table and turned back to her. Silence, laced with heightened anticipation, surrounded them in the small kitchen. Her lungs struggled for air as Scott crossed the small divide between them, his green eyes flashing with determination in the soft candle-light. With tender care, he placed his arms around her, gently coaxing her to him. She thought her legs would soon give out if she let him hold her a second longer, and she loved it. This was what it was like to be safe, protected, cherished.

"Something else Gram said," that low timber in his voice wrapped around her like a ribbon, tying him to her even more. "She said the way to a man's heart is through his belly. I couldn't agree more. Do you know why?"

Shaking her head was her only option at this point. Despite the silly phrase, he was exuding all the things that were opposite of silly.

"Because when it is made with love, a man knows it. You knew just what I needed tonight, and I don't even think you realize it."

Her throat tightened, causing words to catch in her throat as her eyes began to blur with emotion. She hadn't thought about it much when she was planning the meal, but something inside her told her that the comfort of home would be exactly what he needed.

His calloused hand cupped her cheek and he took in each feature of her face. When his gaze stopped at her lips and moved back to her eyes, she knew exactly what was next. And she welcomed it.

With great reverence, his lips met hers, branding her with his peppermint kisses. No words had to be spoken for her to hear his heart.

You mean the world to me.

There is nothing you could do to make me hate you.

I love you.

All too soon, he broke the connection. Her head spun so she buried her face in his shirt. Her heart raced in tandem with the rhythm of his.

An unseemly rumble from his stomach interrupted their moment, breaking the tension between them. Neither could keep from laughing.

He began to move to leave the embrace, but she held tight.

She'd invited him here to talk, but after a kiss like that, she knew it wouldn't take much to explain.

She knew she had his attention again when he moved his hands down her arms and took hold of her hands.

"I just want you to know…"

"I already do," he placed a soft kiss on her forehead.

"I need to say it though." Beth entwined their fingers to keep his focus.

"I know I have been rather confusing since I arrived, and I'm sorry. Being here, in this place, and spending time with you, has been the best kind of medicine. The laughter, the care, the love has given me a wholeness that I've never known. I came down here to find my own way in life, and instead I found my faith in humankind and in God while in your care." She let go of one of his hands, moving it to his unshaven face. "Scott, now that I have this completeness, I never want to let that go."

A sheen formed over his eyes. "Then let's see where this thing will lead us. Having you here has brought something familiar back into my life. I don't feel like a lone bull shark without a family of his own to protect and care for. You have given me something to look forward to, something more than a hot meal, and I couldn't ask God for anything better than to have you back in my life."

Streams of tears traveled down each of their faces. The back of Scott's hand brushed her tears away with tender care then moved to her neck, sending shivers down her spine. He tilted his head just a bit, leaning in for another kiss. Until the beauty of the moment was broken by another growl from his tummy.

She felt a chuckle vibrate under her hand that was placed on his chest. "Are you hungry, Mr. Anderson?" she teased.

"I fear my stomach is reaching for my backbone right now."

Laughter at the moment surrounded them. Before they parted ways, he gave her a quick peck on the lips, intensifying the heat on her face she was already feeling.

Just as they bowed their heads to pray, Scott's phone rang. Looking up to meet her eyes, he pulled the phone from his pocket, concern flashing when he noted the name on the screen.

"This is Scott...Okay...Do you need me at the station now?... Hold on, let me ask," Scott put the phone in his lap. "It's Blake. They have a lead on your brake line, and they think it is connected to the fire on the ferry. Are you able to go over to Savannah with me Tuesday?"

"Yes, of course."

"She said yes. What time? Perfect. I'll see you then."

After ending the call, he moved to hold her chair out for her. Once he sat down at the head of the table beside her, he took hold of her hand. They bowed their heads as they asked God's blessing on the meal.

A different kind of prayer invaded Beth's thoughts. Lord, it would be the best gift if this mess is over by Christmas.

$\mathcal{S}$cott couldn't keep from smiling as various strains of Beth's off-key vocal attempts assaulted the air. She loved that song they played on the radio. He'd never heard it before. He tended to turn off the songs he didn't know, but he wouldn't discourage the joy she clearly felt at this moment. For the first time since she arrived on the island, she looked happy, despite everything that was happening to her.

"Now boarding for Hilton Head, South Carolina. Please move all vehicles ahead slowly. The waters are a little choppy this morning, so we are going to ask all riders to exit the vehicles once they are parked and make their way to the top deck."

Beth's eyes shot wide and all joy left her. "That's ominous, don't you think?"

"It just means they need to take extra precaution. With us being on the deck, if something does happen, at least we won't be trapped in our vehicles."

"Oh, no, it makes sense, but it isn't reassuring by any means."

"No, but we'll be just fine. We're in good hands." Scott placed his hand on hers and gave it a squeeze, hoping it was reassuring.

He was just delighted for the opportunity to show her the affection he'd held back for so long.

Once every car was parked, all the riders made their way, en masse, to the deck above. Scott waited for the narrow aisles to clear before he went over to help Beth out of the truck.

The ride to the mainland was not smooth, which they expected, but even as seafaring as he was, Scott's stomach turned a bit. He tried all the tricks and there was no keeping the rolling stomach away.

"Please tell me this will end soon?" Beth's tone told him she was feeling just as green.

"Soon."

"Why would they still run when the waters are like this?"

"I know for a landlubber, ye think tis the worst it'll get. I'll turn ye into the Queen of the Sea, soon enough," Scott informed in his best pirate voice.

Beth started to laugh. "That was terrible."

"Yep, it was." *But you're not thinking about how terrible this ride is.*

A woman a couple of seats behind them began to yell while one of the crew members attempted to calm her. Scott looked to see if he could help in any way, only to see the woman was Valerie.

"Oh boy."

"I don't even have to look to know it is her," Beth whispered. "I wonder why she is going to Hilton Head."

"None of our business. Just focus on the horizon, love."

"You mean the one that is bouncing?" He noticed the softness of her features when he glanced at her. "I like that nickname better."

Scott wrapped an arm around her shoulders and pulled her to him. It was comforting, the way she nestled into his side. He had wanted to call her something more endearing for weeks, but without permission, he hadn't risked it.

"I like it as well."

Throughout the rest of the trip, Scott did his best to keep Beth talking in an effort to keep both of their minds off the rocky trip. As long as they held onto each other, blocking out everything going on around them, the sick feeling disappeared.

In no time, the ferry ride was over, and Scott was pulling onto the road to Savannah. Just like on the deck of the boat, Beth nuzzled in beside him instead of by the passenger door. She looped her arm through his. Everything was right in the world, as far as he was concerned.

When they pulled into the police department, Scott saw a familiar red Ferrari in the parking lot.

"How did she get here before us?" Beth clearly noticed it as well.

"I'm not sure but I get the feeling we are about to find out."

They were ushered into separate rooms, and the fear in Beth's eyes was unmistakable. He tried to reassure her as best as possible. *Divide and conquer?*

A detective entered the room, placed a manila folder on the table and took a seat. He didn't introduce himself or inform Scott why he was here. As he thumbed through the file, a knock sounded on the door and a clerk walked in with two cups of coffee.

"Would you like any cream or sugar, Mr. Anderson?"

"No, thank you. I'm good."

The young man nodded and left the room.

"Mr. Anderson, I am Detective Jones. Detective Andrews had to turn this case over to me due to his connection with you. It wasn't a problem when he was looking into things for your friend, but he has to remain neutral with you. Understand?"

"I do. It is good to know he is still helping Beth."

"Yes, well, let's talk about your case." Detective Jones pushed record on the player and began by telling Scott he could have an attorney present if he wished. Not that he was in trouble, but for his protection.

For two hours, the detective drilled Scott with question after question, many times asking the same thing but in various ways. Scott figured it was to see if the story was consistent. For not being the one in trouble, he sure felt like he was sitting in his dad's office waiting for judgement to fall. He could only remind himself that the officer was simply doing his job.

Then came the question, "Mr. Anderson, do you know a Daniel Black?"

"No."

"Do you know Valerie Hornigold?"

Scott froze.

"Yes," he drew the word out. What had she done?

"Do you know Charles Ainsley?"

Scott bowed his head in disbelief. He knew now what happened to his freighter.

"Yes."

"Did you work for him in any capacity?"

"I volunteer on Merriweather Island in service to the community, but I was asked to do so by Mr. Ainsley."

"Did he ever ask you to do anything that you felt was outside of the bounds in which you were hired?"

"Yes."

At his answer, the detective's white bushy eyebrows shot up. "Care to explain?"

Scott proceeded to explain the conversation in Ainsley's office as well as the mistreatment of Sarah Reid.

"And did the incidents that occurred to Miss Stevens and yourself follow after?"

"Yes."

"Well, Mr. Anderson, I think we have what we need to proceed. We will be in contact soon."

The detective stood and Scott followed suit, taking the

extended hand and shaking it. "Thank you, sir, for your help. Who should I call if there are any more incidents?"

"Just call your local sheriff's office. He should be able to help."

"All right, then. Thank you."

He met Beth in the hall as they followed an officer out of the station. Once in the truck, they both sighed.

"Hey! What are you two kids doing?" Jacob's baritone voice boomed in Scott's chest and pulled a squeal out of Beth.

"Jake, what do you want?" a round of chuckles followed the silliness.

"We are throwing a surprise baby shower tonight for Liz. Co-ed and all. Since you guys are here, stick around and join us. We'd love to see you there."

Scott looked to Beth and knew he didn't need to ask. "I think we can do that. I have to pick up parts for her Bronco anyway."

"Great, I'll see you there." Jacob smacked the door and jogged back into the station.

"Today is becoming a day for the two of us. Now that the business with the police is over, it's like a day-long date. I like that," Beth chimed, her face alight with excitement. "And getting the parts to fix the brakes, double bonus. I've missed working."

Scott had experienced many fun and exciting days throughout the course of his life, but the days that he spent with Beth were the ones he enjoyed the most. Her infectious laughter and her crazy antics made the most mundane activity fun.

"Can we do a little memory lane sightseeing? I haven't spent any time here since I was sixteen."

"Your wish is my command. Let's do it."

He took her to all of their favorite spots—The Waving Girl, Bonaventure Cemetery, The Mercer-Williams House, and lastly, Forsyth Park where they ordered sandwiches at the park cafe.

"I've always loved this park. There is nothing like it in Michigan."

"I'm sure you have beautiful parks and sights.. I wouldn't mind going up there some day, to see the places and people who shaped you."

"Oh, you don't want to do that. It would mean spending time with my family. Trust me."

"Well, what about your dad? I'd like a chance to talk to him at least. Someday."

Beth whipped her head in his direction with enough force that he was sure he felt the breeze created by her ponytail. "Why would you want to talk to my dad?" The worry in her voice only made him laugh.

"Don't read too much into it. I would just like to get to know the man."

Her relief was evident by the sigh that escaped her lips. "Well, I still like this park most. The moss, the trees, the people, and that fountain—it all makes this town breathtaking."

"You should see it in the spring. The azaleas and magnolias are beautiful."

"I bet it's a beautiful location for a wedding."

Scott inhaled at the comment, sucking a piece of his sandwich down the wrong tube, causing a coughing fit.

Beth began patting his back. "Are you okay?"

"Yup. Let's head to the baby shower." Scott needed to get away from where this conversation was taking them. "We can stop at the store for a gift."

"And diapers. You can never have enough diapers with a newborn. At least that is what I hear."

When the baby purchases were made, and the brake line safely rested on the floor behind him, Scott took the long way to Bluff Drive in Isle of Hope just to hear Beth make little sounds of wonder.

"Haven't you ever been here before?"

"No. We came to the island and that was it."

As he approached the street, two park benches sat on the

bank of the Skidaway River in front of them. An ancient oak's limbs spread out over the benches while Spanish moss hung low. He heard her whisper beside him, so he rounded the bend as slowly as possible just so she could savor the moment.

Park benches, personal docks with boats ready for fishing and fun, and kids running in the single lane road brought to life the little community with a view to die for.

"I want to live here. I mean, who wouldn't? Look at these homes and the view. Don't tell me this is where the brothers live."

"Okay, I won't."

Scott pulled into the fifth house and a groan escaped Beth's beautiful lips. "Oh, that's just not fair. Look at that house."

He couldn't help but smile at the awe and wonder in her voice as she admired the home and its surroundings. The Antebellum home with the ancient oak in the front yard and perfectly landscaped yard was the epitome of charming southern architecture.

Scott climbed out of the truck and walked to her side to let her out. When he opened the door, she was still going on about beauty of the home and how "it could only be more beautiful on the inside."

Ready to have a relaxing evening with friends, he held out his hand to her. "Let's go inside so you can find out for yourself. The people that live here aren't too bad either." He was sure she would find an extended family here like he had.

Family doesn't always mean blood relation.

26

"I really liked that family. They were so nice and hospitable and fun as all get out." Beth had never known an entire family to love the Lord and each other so much that the love poured out onto everyone they touched. "And Mama Andrews? Oh, Scott, she is a gem of a woman." She recalled the woman's embrace as Beth walked through the front door, the memory bringing tears to her eyes. "It was like hugging Gram."

Scott watched the road ahead as he nodded in agreement. "I have gotten the same feeling before. It's like when she hugs you, everything about her wraps around you."

"Yes. Just like that."

"Did you hear what she said about Gram when I told her Gram's real name?"

"No, what did she say?"

"She and Gram are second cousins. She told me *all* the details, but I'm too tired to remember right now." A yawn fought for escape from her mouth, "I also get silly and chatty. I don't know why…"

Scott's hand reached across the truck, unbuckled her seatbelt and wrapped around her waist, pulling her to his side. "Hey Beth? Shhhhh."

"Sorry," she whispered with a giggle as she buckled the lap belt.

Beth tucked herself in tight under Scott's protective arm as the bridge to Merriweather Island came into focus. Though the day had been long, the party fun, and the sights still the most beautiful she'd ever seen, Merriweather was home. Michigan was nice, but right now, despite Scott's desire to see the Great Lakes State, she didn't care to ever return. Maybe that would change with time. A piece of her hoped it would. Discord within the family was not something she desired for her loved ones. Especially when Gram's words of wisdom constantly played in her head.

You have to love them, sugar. No one said you have to like their behavior.

That was what she would do. She'd learn to forgive and let go. Forgetting may never happen, but she could work on forgiveness.

At last, her cottage came into view. It was her cottage, not Gram's, not the island's, but hers and hers alone. It was now her job to care for and preserve the rich history that it encapsulated for future generations.

Scott pulled into the driveway but instead of stopping in front, he went toward the edge of the cliff, turning off the headlights. A chilled breeze blew through the lowered windows, making her shiver and tuck in tighter yet into Scott's side.

"I should roll the windows up, so you don't freeze, but I like having you here like this," he squeezed her.

"I'll stay put," she cooed. Now that she was discovering how having a relationship with him could be, she had no interest in running away.

The dark surrounded them as the stars flickered overhead. Scott turned on the radio but left the volume low as music filled the cab of the truck. A song from the mid-nineties came on, bringing a smile to her face. She was only a kid the first time she heard it, but it sparked a memory of when she first met Scott.

"Do you remember when we first met?"

"I sure do. You had braided pigtails, braces, and the cutest freckles across your nose," he grazed a finger down the slope of her nose, sending shivers through her. "How old were you?"

"I think I was thirteen. I was such a dork."

"Yeah, but we all were at that age."

Moments passed and as the song begged to let the guy "be the one," Beth couldn't miss the resemblance to Scott's own plea. He wanted to be the one to take care of her, to make her laugh and to hold her when she cried. Who wouldn't want that kind of safety?

"I fell for you that first day," Scott confessed, but his voice was so quiet she almost missed it.

"My first day here? In August?"

"No, the first day we met. As kids."

"How? I was..." a finger landed on her lips, halting her from her self-degradation.

"I know what you were, and I liked you then. Don't you get it? Through the awkward phases, the crazy moments, and the years that kept us apart—I have thought of you, cared for you, and loved you."

Beth let his words sink into her heart as she processed the gravity of them. He had always loved her. Even when she may not have been lovable. She searched her memory for when she first saw him as more than just a nice boy.

"I think it was the second summer for me. You sat with me on the cliff here while my parents fought inside. Gram, I know, did her best to smooth things over, so that we weren't caught in the middle. You rode your bike up. I guess you saw me sitting there crying. You walked up to me and sat down wrapping an arm around me. That was when you went from 'just a nice boy' to my protector and best friend."

"Just a friend?" he teased.

"By the end of that summer, if you'd asked me to be your girl, I would have said yes. You won me over then like you did now with your gentle ways and teasing manner. Your love sealed the deal for me. The way you love is unlike anything I have seen in my entire life. I tried to find it in other boys after my last summer here but never found it. I guess I just gave up, figuring it was a fluke."

"I guess I didn't realize it was so special. I just loved you the way I saw my dad love my mom. Now, I think much of it had to do with not wanting to miss a moment with someone I love. My mom was dad's everything on Earth. Her death changed him in many different ways. Their years were too short and when I noticed that she wasn't much older than I am now, I felt like time was wasting away, like her."

"So, you got a little pushy." She teased with a light jab in his ribs. "I see it now. I'm okay with it, though."

"I'm glad you understand."

Talking ceased as Scott cupped her face with one hand and ran his thumb along her cheek. His face drew near as her heart began to race in anticipation, but then he stopped. A smirk appeared on his handsome face.

The blissful agony in waiting for that blessed kiss grew to unbearable heights as she ran her hand up his chest and around his neck. "I wish you would hurry it up."

He teased with a,"Yes, dear," as his lips met hers.

She was swept away by this kind-hearted pirate. He promised to give her the space she needed to find the freedom she wanted but would be by her side, loving her, through it all.

For in her search for independence she found something too scrumptious to leave behind.

Journal Entry

Christmas Day

These past few weeks have been blissfully busy with Scott and Comfort Cuisine. Once the brakes were fixed, I was back in business and it's booming. The community support here on Merriweather has been touching.

They arrested Mr. Ainsley and Mr. Black for the fires, but they had a difficult time making charges stick for cutting my brake lines. At this point, I'm just glad that Mr. Ainsley will no longer be the mayor. Some are asking Scott to run, but he told me that he has little interest in the office.

Daddy called to wish me a Merry Christmas this morning and gave me the update on mother and rest of the family. I missed him today but not as much as I thought I should. Same with mother, Barbra and Catherine. Maybe the hurt is still too deep.

I've enjoyed this freedom, but I have also discovered bits and pieces of who I really am. Here are a few things, so I don't forget.

1.) I love the warmer weather. Snow is nice, but sand between the toes is better.

2.) I hate crowds but love people. I know, it doesn't make sense, but I understand it. Being inside the food trailer gives me a safety wall between me and them, making it possible to interact normally.

3.) I really, really like spending time with Scott. He is all I first imagined him to be and then some. The best moments with him are at the end of the day, when we are sitting on the deck of his houseboat or on the bench near the cliff here at the cottage. I don't know what's in store for us, but I am looking forward to the journey.

Sad that this story is over? Don't be, there is more to come. Keep an eye out for the continuation of Scott and Beth's story in *Heart Pressed* set on the backdrop of Elnora Island. Meet Dante and Amara, heirs of rival wineries on the island who see a little more in each other than an enemy. Unfortunately, their families' bitterness runs deep, causing plenty of problems of the people of Elnora and possibly for Scott and Beth.

Heart Pressed Coming February 2021

Until then, be sure to check out all the other Merriweather Island books in the Independence Island Series.

GRANDMA'S CONEY ISLAND SAUCE

(I will admit that I am not sure where she got this recipe. I believe it is a combination of the Original Flint's Coney Island Sauce and Angelo's Coney Island Sauce. Something my grandma Apsey concocted in the 60's or 70's, maybe sooner.)

1tbs. Oleo

1tbs. Cooking Oil

2 medium onions chopped fine

1/2tsp. Garlic powder

1tbs. Salt & Pepper

2tbs. Chili Powder

1tbs. Mustard

1 1/2lbs. Hamburger

6oz. Tomato sauce

6oz. Water

(Or 12oz. Tomato juice to replace sauce and water)

5 Hot dogs ground fine (Kogel Vienna's are best)

Simmer for 3 hours

Skim some of the fat off

Serve over hot dogs and top with onions, mustard, ketchup,

or cheese sauce. Whatever you like. Or you can just Package &
Freeze

ABOUT THE AUTHOR

Melissa Wardwell resides in Corunna, Michigan with her husband and three children, all of whom they home school. Besides writing, she enjoys reading, taking photos, and motorcycle rides with her husband. Her hope is that each story touches your heart, gives you hope or just gives you a moment away from the chaos of life.

- facebook.com/mwardwellwrites
- twitter.com/mwardwellwrites
- instagram.com/mwardwellwrites
- bookbub.com/authors/melissa-wardwell

ALSO BY MELISSA WARDWELL

Promises from Above

What God Brings Together (Book One)

A Christmas Wedding

Dance and be Glad

I Know the Plans

Books in Savannah

Finding Hope in Savannah

Hope Beyond the Shore

OTHER BOOKS IN THE MERRIWEATHER ISLAND SERIES

Dual Power of Convenience (Book One) by Chautona Havig

Secret Beach Boyfriend (Book Three) by Kari Trumbo

Her Merriweather Hero (Book Four) by Rachel Skatvold

Mishaps Off the Mainland (Book Five) by Tabitha Bouldin

Restoring Fairhaven (Book Six) by Carolyn Miller

SECRET BEACH BOYFRIEND

MERRIWEATHER ISLAND BOOK THREE
SNEAK PEEK

KARI TRUMBO

1

*A*nnie Roman squinted into the bright setting sun to the ferry pulling into the dock. All that rushing around on board didn't look relaxing. The bustling ship, packed with vacationers and islanders, seemed to approach at a snail's crawl from her safe little booth on the shore. A stiff breeze blew in off the Atlantic, and she held onto her floppy straw hat as the ferry pulled in and prepared to dock on Mimosa Island. The same as it did every day, bringing islanders and vacationers alike to the Independence Island chain. Even from the protection of her booth, the wind threatened to whip her hat away.

A businessman in a narrow cut, slate gray suit caught her eye as he adjusted his tie on his way toward her booth. Men like him were unusual on the islands. He strode toward her with his head stuck in his phone, his thumbs moving at breakneck speed. That was different. Since people needed to work long hours for jobs requiring suits, islanders typically didn't take those positions. Vacationers didn't don suits to head to the island. It was over an hour ride by ferry to the mainland, not optimal if someone had to work longer than eight hours a day.

He'd almost reached her booth when a family of eight jostled in ahead of him like a motorboat blasting into a slip. Mom looked to have already been in the sun a few hours too long. Her hair hung clumped together in sections around her damp face, and her forehead resembled the inside of a watermelon.

"Where do we go to find the hotel?" The woman was laden with suitcases, seemingly attached to her by the force of nature alone. Her clothing pulled where all the luggage dug at her shoulders and arms. Her sunglasses had to have been sat upon at some point.

The mother shrugged her bags to the ground then leaned against the booth. "Um…which hotel, miss?"

Annie always tried to be nice, but there were many places for vacationers to stay on the large island. Most Independence islanders worked on Mimosa in those parks, attractions, and hotels.

The woman sighed loudly and one of her children screamed, "Ice cream!" and dashed into the crowd toward a street vendor's cart. Annie had long since tuned out the crank music box sound of the ice cream man.

The woman's husband dropped all the bags he'd been lugging and gave chase as she pointed to one of her other children to stand guard over the bags, giving him one of those threatening mom-looks that Annie recognized immediately as "harried traveling mom."

The man in the suit moved forward. "Excuse me, I'm in a little bit of a hurry. I need to get to Merriweather Island, and I can't find a schedule. Not even online. I can't remember which ferry is the one that takes the long way around the islands and which is the direct route."

Annie wanted to answer him, it would only take a moment and he had been there first. As she opened her mouth, the mother shuffled him to the side and yanked a brochure out of her gargantuan flamingo colored purse. "This one, right here." She pointed with threatening staccato to a red X on a map of the island, like a treasure map. There were no street names and few landmarks other than scattered tourist traps. Instead of looking at the map, she searched the corners of the page for a logo. It looked like a brochure a hotel might give out as a draw for customers. She bit her lip and tried to think clearly. Though she worked the ferry booth, she wasn't well-versed on where everything was on Mimosa, especially under pressure. The line behind the suited man lengthened as she tried to figure out where to send the woman.

"I think you go down this street and take the third right. That's what it looks like on the map."

The woman rolled her eyes. "Listen here, miss 'I don't care about the tourist,' I could've figured *that* out on my own." She stomped away.

Just another reason why we don't need tourism on the other islands...

"You're welcome," Annie mumbled aloud.

The man in the suit frowned as the ferry he probably should've stayed on pulled away. "Can you help me now?" He'd put his phone away, and he held a small shoulder bag in one hand. His sunglasses were designer, but he didn't have an attitude like she'd expected based on what he wore. What she could see of his face was handsome and tanned. He didn't smile or remove his sunglasses as he stepped closer to her booth.

"I'm sorry. I hope you aren't in too much—" she tried to answer as another eager tourist shoved forward.

"Excuse me!" An old man in a Hawaiian print shirt slapped his hands down on her counter. This part of the job always made her uncomfortable. She had to try to make both people happy. Yet, how could she?

"I was helping this gentleman..."

"But I need to know right now, is there a tour of the light-house on Breakers Head? How do we even *get* to the other islands...swim? I've gone up and down the coast and I can see

189

the other island here on this map, but I can't find a way to get to it." He crossed his arms and glared at her as if he were accusing her of personally hiding the secret.

She was used to people treating her like she wasn't really a person, just an information booth. No more feelings than Google. Today was no different than any other. This job was the reason she lived in a tiny cottage by the shore...on the far side of Merriweather where she couldn't even see another island. She clenched her jaw to keep from saying what she'd like to.

Mr. Suit laid his hands on the counter of her booth and stared over at the older man. "There are no tours available on any of the other islands. Probably never will be. You're free to swim if you'd like, but you won't find much on the other islands besides beaches. Just warn the coast guard before you do. Now, I've been waiting, can I please talk to..." He glanced at her and his eye caught for just a moment on the silly pirate map nametag with a giant X that her boss insisted she wear. "Annie, here? Please?"

The older man stalked off and though his mouth moved, she couldn't hear anything he said over the wind. Mr. Suit had to have come from the islands or at least be familiar with them if he knew none of the rest had any offerings for tourists. But she didn't recognize him, which was strange since she'd lived there her whole life. There was no way he could've guessed about the other islands. Who'd ever heard of islands without tourism? But that's exactly what her parents had always loved about this particular archipelago. Mimosa was their offering to the world, the place anyone was welcome. The other islands were God's little gift to the people who inhabited them.

"You're an islander?" Or perhaps the relative of an islander...

He finally took off his sunglasses, but it didn't help. She still didn't recognize him. His hair was too caramel to be blond and too light to be brown. When he smiled, he had those long dimples that framed his whole lips. "Not for a decade. So long, I don't remember my way around anymore. I hope I didn't steer him wrong. My parents never told me the association changed the rules. I would think they would've said something." He set down his bag and shoved his hands in his pockets. Standing like that, with the sun shining on his face and the ocean in the background, he looked like a men's suit model.

People behind him started thinning out as they actually took out maps of the island. She was at a loss for words. He was nothing like any other islander. "Nope, still no tourism anywhere but Mimosa. You said you wanted to go to...Merriweather?" That was her island. While it wasn't as small as Hopper or Sparrow, it was small enough that she thought she knew everyone there.

"Rafe Tedfield." He smiled. "And yes, Merriweather."

She knew the Tedfields and knew they had a son who was a few years older than her, but since she'd been homeschooled, she'd missed a generation. She knew people older than her who were her parents' friends and younger, but few cohorts, especially the male ones.

The next boat that would take him would be the same one she would be taking home. He could've stayed on the main ferry and made it, but it tended to lumber along. There always seemed to be people hopping from island to island and willing to give rides, not to mention the bridges between most islands, but there was no bridge from Mimosa.

"The afternoon ferry leaves in about an hour from that dock." Curiosity got the better of her because the Tedfields were her Bible study partners and she would be meeting with them later tonight. "Mark and Gail didn't mention you'd be coming." They hadn't mentioned much of anything lately with all the bickering.

His façade of indifference cracked for a moment and his forehead rippled with worry lines. "My visit is more of a surprise. One of many, I hope." He smiled, slipped his sunglasses back on and nodded in thanks as he strode off into the crowd.

That floppy hat was unmistakable. From Rafe's position seated at the rail of the ferry, he could see just about everyone, including the woman from the ferry ticket booth. Annie had been her name. The hat was smart, he'd forgotten how the sun beat down on the boat as if the ocean was glass. His suit would need to go to the cleaners when he got back to Savannah.

Annie had said she knew his parents, which meant she'd probably seen the trouble brewing between them. His phone buzzed and he slipped the device from his pocket. The text from his mother was short and to the point, *I'm finished with this. I can't take it anymore.*

His heart clenched. He couldn't be this close to home and have her walk out. Not now. He'd come as quickly as he could. Getting time off wasn't easy when he was the finance department of the dealership where he worked. He never took time off. His fingers flew over the screen. *Just hold on, Mom. We'll talk soon. Don't do anything yet.*

If he told her he was within a mile of her, she'd freak and try to clean the whole house in twenty minutes. His mom had always suffered from minor OCD, which was part of the issue. Growing up, it had been manageable. He'd just kept his friends and everyone else away from the house because a disturbance in Mom's schedule could trigger a few weeks of stress for her. His dad had mentioned over the last few months she was getting more sensitive and he didn't know how to deal with it. No matter how he tried, it was always wrong. The OCD seemed to ebb and flow like the tide, but Dad could never see it coming. What they needed was counseling, and a miracle. That's why

Rafe had told his boss he was finally taking time off so he could be there.

His boss hadn't been pleased but couldn't do much. Rafe hadn't taken a vacation day in years and who else his age didn't even take mental health days? He'd built a huge amount of trust with the owner of the dealership. However, taking too long on the island could jeopardize his whole career.

There wouldn't be time to get to know the woman from the ferry booth, no matter how enjoyable that might be. Annie sat huddled with her back to the wind, her nose buried in a book. The bag at her feet was plain brown paper with sturdy handles that read *The Book Barrow* in scrolling letters. She was the only person on the ferry even close to his age and everyone else seemed to ignore her. So many people on the islands were older or retired. He assumed all his friends had left, just as he had, to find jobs on the mainland. That had been their plan at graduation, though he'd call later to find out. He loved Merriweather, but it just didn't have everything he needed, like a midnight taco once in a while.

The ferry pulled into the slip by Pirate's Cove, and after it docked, they dropped the apron. Annie seemed to sense where they were, and she carefully put her bookmark in and dropped the book in her bag. He stayed back a good distance. No sense in making her think he was following her. The island was small enough that she'd probably think he was anyway.

He let a few older residents off before him. They nodded his way but didn't speak. If they knew who he was, they probably thought it was well-past time for him to come home and help his family. Course, he could just be projecting. He'd been known to do that too. The whole island seemed to now know about his mother's issue, whereas they'd kept it private when he was young. From what he'd gathered from his father's texts, they'd been to a Bible study and the leader had tried to give them counsel. It wasn't helping.

Rafe waited his turn, then disembarked. The tangy smell of beach hit him first. The sensory history sank in for just a minute as he let the scent bring him back. He didn't have much time, but he hadn't been on the island in a decade. His parents had always come to visit him for holidays, and he hadn't made coming back a priority.

A row of older, colorless buildings was all he could see of Merriweather proper. Even ten years before, the downtown had people. Now, there were no cars parked along the street, nor people walking down the sidewalk. Only people making their way to the small parking area along the port.

With so few businesses, he'd have to brew his own coffee in the morning – if his mom let him get a coffee pot dirty. A large truck with a trailer rumbled to the parking area and stopped. He couldn't read the side of it from where he stood, but people immediately changed directions and headed for the truck. A dark-haired woman climbed down and headed for the back. Within minutes, the side of the truck was open and taking orders. He smiled at all the people waiting for the convenience food. He'd never wanted the islanders to give up their independence, but it was nice to see people trying to make this lifestyle work for everyone.

He breathed in deeply and listened to the gulls call as he made his way up the slight incline past the cove. A couple people stared at him, but they didn't say a word. He wasn't dressed for the occasion and ten years changed a person a lot, especially if those ten years started on graduation day. He loosened his tie until it hung loosely around his neck and fought the urge to yank his phone from his pocket to check the time.

A quick scan of the area and Rafe realized he'd lost Annie. He'd hoped to at least wave before she drove off, since she'd known he was coming to Merriweather. At least he'd see her again when he headed back to work in a few days. Hopefully, that was all it took to get his parents back on speaking terms.

Mom and Dad's Bible study was supposed to be that evening but if they were fighting, they might not go. That would give him time to talk sense into them that very night. He couldn't remember when the study started exactly, but he'd have to catch them before they left, just in case. He chuckled as he strode along in the setting sun. He was on island time now; the study would start when everyone arrived. That was just the way of things.

Once he'd reached the top of the slope leading up to town, he veered right and headed down the road toward home. A tiny two-seater car that was small enough to park sideways in the road pulled to a stop alongside him. Annie waved from the driver's seat.

The window slowly slid down. "Hey, I know the way and it's a long walk, especially in a suit. Want a ride? I've got air conditioning…" She laughed, looking much more at ease than she had in her booth.

He tugged on his collar as sweat trickled down his back. He could walk, but a ride would be much easier, and that AC was more than welcome. Plus, if a pretty woman asked him for a ride, who was he to say no? He nodded and she popped open the trunk from her spot in the driver's seat. He laughed as he realized that trunk wouldn't even fit four bags of groceries comfortably. Luckily, he hadn't packed much. He shut the trunk and got in next to her, already more comfortable as a blast of cool air hit him.

"Where did you get this little ride? Not on the islands." Even Mimosa didn't have a dealership.

"I ordered it online. You can get just about anything these days. The dealership sent a man over and I signed my life away. I needed a car that was smaller than my house." She laughed nervously.

Smaller? He glanced behind him at the rear window and held in a laugh. The car was so small if he were any taller, he wouldn't fit, and he wasn't a big guy. As they took the road that that circled the island, he took a moment to really look at Annie. She had dark golden hair with a slight wave to it. Her face was natural, without any hint of makeup. She was the kind of girl he would've hung out with before he'd decided his career was more important than marriage. The kind who could be distracting. But maybe he would need something positive if his parents proved to be a more difficult project than he thought.

The gravel road led them along the east side of the island and finally to the south-easternmost point where there was more sand and scattered homes than anything else. A white two-story house sat on a man-made rise about fifty yards from the sandy shore. The house where he'd grown up hadn't changed a bit. He'd loved to climb down the high rock wall to get to the water, when he knew he'd have enough time to clean up before mom would see him. The house wasn't large but looked like a small white barn from the outside. There was a two-level deck off the ocean side of the house, the upper one was from his parents' room, the lower one led into the living room. When he was growing up, they'd repainted the outside every five years because wind and storm rain would chip away at the paint fast. It looked like it needed to be done. Probably one more task that was irritating Mom.

"I'm sure I'll see you around." Annie clutched the steering wheel and bit her lip like she wanted to say more.

He knew just what she was thinking, even without knowing her. She would want to inform him what he was walking into, in case he didn't realize. "I'm sure you will. Thanks for the ride." He hated to run, but that look of mixed worry and pity sat in his stomach wrong. While he'd like to enlist Annie's help in remaining sane while he was on the island, pity was the last thing he wanted to see on her face.

She popped the trunk once more and he grabbed his bag before striding up to the front door and opening it. He hadn't warned them, but he wasn't prepared for the organized chaos in front of him. Huge stacks of newspapers lined the kitchen walls, but all of them perfect like they'd come right off a printing press and landed there. Clean pans sat nested on the kitchen counter like they'd been pulled right from the box. Six sets of various sized kitchen storage containers stood like soldiers flanking the entire kitchen counter from largest to smallest and back again, creating a cream ceramic wave. All strange, considering his mother had never even allowed a microwave on her kitchen counter, nor was Dad allowed a newspaper subscription because of the mess.

"Mom?" Rafe cleared his throat and leaned to look through the pass-through window to the living room. There was no answer and he gave up the act and tugged his phone from his pocket. It was just after six. He was sure his parents didn't have to be at their study until seven or so. "Dad?"

He heard the living room screen door close and peered down the hall. His father Mark tapped one foot against the other to get the sand off and Rafe flinched, glancing down at his feet. He'd forgotten to remove his shoes.

"Rafe!" His father strode in with arms wide. "I'm so glad you're here. It's good to see you. This is so...unexpected." He didn't miss the worried glance his father gave the whole kitchen.

He wished the deep lines of stress across his father's face actually conveyed the message of welcome.

"It sounded like you and Mom could use some help. I came as quickly as I could." And maybe Mom more than he'd thought. "What's going on?" He gestured to the room at large. He still couldn't believe what he was seeing.

Dad led him to the table, and they sat. "Mom's outside. The waves... They are constant, you know. They help her to calm down when something happens. Problem is, things that never bothered her before suddenly do. I'm at my wits end." He bowed his head and rubbed his forehead. "I don't know what to do when the Lord says no. All my life, I had faith that if you asked for things that would seem to help the Kingdom and the people around you, that He would see fit to bless you."

Rafe straightened his spine and pursed his lips. God was God and he'd do what He wanted. Over the years, planning was the only way to ensure success. What Mom needed was an intervention of both support and help. Where prayer obviously hadn't succeeded, work would. "I'm here for a few weeks to help. Both with Mom's OCD and getting you two back on the same page."

Dad shook his head and the lines on his brow deepened as he craned his neck to glance back over his shoulder. "I think that sun has set, son."

Made in the USA
Middletown, DE
07 January 2024

47428356R00120